THE TANGLED WEB

a novel by

Barbara Hazard

FAWCETT COVENTRY • NEW YORK

THE TANGLED WEB

Published by Fawcett Coventry Books, a unit of CBS Publications, the Consumer Publishing Division of CBS Inc.

Copyright © 1981 by Barbara Hazard

All Rights Reserved

ISBN: 0-449-50177-9

Printed in the United States of America

First Fawcett Coventry printing: April 1981

10 9 8 7 6 5 4 3 2 1

*O what a tangled web we weave,
When first we practice to deceive!*

          Sir Walter Scott
          1771–1832

ONE

"But I don't want a season!"

The intense hush that greeted this heartfelt sentiment was not so much one of respect for the speaker's vehement words as it was a silence of complete shock. Lady Winship paused in the act of raising her napkin to her lips, and her brother James put down his coffee cup with a snap that threatened the second-best china. For a moment, the only sound was that of the cold rain pattering on the windowpanes of the breakfast room where the three were sitting. Lady Winship lowered her napkin and stared at her daughter, her fair brows knitting together in a frown.

"You do not want a season, Mariel?" she asked, her soft musical voice faintly disbelieving. "Why ever not?"

Mariel Winship stirred her coffee restlessly. "Oh, Mama, what would be the use? I don't want to be dressed in the height of fashion all the time and have to go to balls and parties and make silly conversation with some gentleman who would rather be riding, as I would myself, instead of sipping tea and uttering inanities! It... it seems such a waste of time!"

This somewhat incoherent description of the glories of a London season that most young girls looked forward to so eagerly appeared to stun Lady Winship into silence again. Her brother poured another cup of coffee for himself and stared solemnly at his niece. He was a taciturn man, pondering long before committing himself to an opinion. His sister and his niece dearly loved him, although to a casual observer his countenance appeared both severe and threatening. Where his sister was blond and fragile with startling light green eyes and a delicate complexion, he was tall and blockish, his dark hair and beard and a formidable pair of eyebrows making him seem almost ferocious. He continued to stare at his niece, his brow furrowed in thought. Mariel, who had been christened Mary Ellen Winship, favored neither her uncle nor her mother, although she had inherited her mother's green eyes. Instead of the beautiful oval face, hers showed the square jawline of the Winships, and Lady Winship's classical profile had not repeated, for Mariel's nose had a definite tilt and was covered with golden freckles to boot. Her hair was thick and completely unruly where Lady Winship's curled charmingly around her brow, and to complete the picture, Mariel's blond hair had distinct reddish tones instead of the pure golden shade of her mother's. Mariel called it "carroty," but as she was completely unconcerned about her appearance, her looks did not distress her; there were too many other things of more importance to think about!

Uncle James rose from the table, and Mariel asked quickly, "Do you go to the lochfield, uncle? May I join you? I am so anxious to see how the lambing is coming along!"

James glanced quickly at his sister, still sitting at the table pleating her napkin in distraction. Mariel had followed him around the farm since she was big enough to keep up with his long strides, but he knew her vehement denial of a trip to London had upset her mother, and he felt the girl should stay and let Ellen have a further chance to extol the glories of a season in town. As he looked at her inquiringly, she glanced up and colored a little.

"Oh, it is all right, James! She may go with you, although why anyone would want to trudge all over a wet field in this rain and mud is more than I can understand!"

Mariel jumped up and whirled around to her mother's chair to hug her heartily. "Poor mama! Not only is your only child a stay-at-home, she is a farmer at heart! Why wasn't I born a boy? Then no one would think it at all strange for me to like farming, and lambs, and yes, even mud!"

Her uncle barked a laugh and even Lady Winship had to join in ruefully as the two left the room, Mariel's eager questions echoing in the hall.

Dugan came in to see if anything more would be required before he began his morning's work. Although James MacDonald was a well-to-do squire, there was no show of indoor servants or luxury. He lived austerely, his money going to purchase new stock or for additional acreage for the farm he loved as well as his niece did. "You may clear, Dugan," Lady Winship said with a faint smile for the old man as she left to see Mrs. Dugan in the kitchen to plan the morning chores and the dinner menu. When she had discussed the merits of a rabbit stew and boiled mutton and heard in detail the condition of some of the sheets in the large linen press, she wandered back to the great hall and the cheerful fire blazing there.

It was a pleasant room, made comfortable by her own touches. James would never have thought of covering the large armchairs that flanked the fireplace with dark red linen, nor of polishing the brass andirons and candlesticks so they glowed softly in the firelight, nor would he have had the paintings cleaned of the soot and dirt they had accumulated over the years, nor hung the display of highland weaponry so well on the wall. One dog lay dozing by the hearth, and that only because he was too old and stiff to work the flocks. There were no lap dogs in the MacDonald household. Lady Winship sank down near the fire and opened her mending basket, absently patting the old dog who waved his tail in gratitude. She stared into the flames.

It had been a mistake to come to Scotland all those years ago, she thought drearily, for now Mariel had no desire to be anything but a farmer's wife here in her beloved hills. Oh, she had seen to her upbringing and made sure she spoke without the local dialect, and that she knew the things a young lady must know, but to Mariel, learning to converse politely, or sew a fine seam, or dance easily, had been chores, whereas feeding the stock or helping at the shearing was not. Lady Winship's mending dropped unheeded near her chair as she pondered the problem. As the daughter of Lord Winship, Marquess of Braxton, Mariel could look as high as she pleased for a husband, but if she were determined to bury herself here in Scotland there would be small chance of that. Lady Winship had been very careful to avoid the word "husband," not wishing to frighten her daughter. Well she remembered how horrified she had been at just Mariel's age when she had been informed that Lord Winship had asked for her hand, after meeting her just a few times, and that she was expected to marry before she even had a chance to enjoy herself! She had not loved Lord Winship, considering him one of her father's friends for he was twenty years older than she was, and at seventeen that seemed an insurmountable gulf. But she had married him; what else could she do? There was no setting yourself up against your parents' wishes in those days, she thought. Imagine if she had had the courage to say, as Mariel had this morning, "But I don't *want* to!" She smiled faintly. She would never have dared to speak so to her formidable father and austere mother. Both she and her sisters had married as their parents arranged, and if she could not vouch for their marriages, she knew that hers had not had time to mature to the point where she could have said it was either success or failure. She had found herself pregnant on her honeymoon, to Lord Winship's delight. Abruptly curtailing their tour of Greece, he had taken her home to Braxton to await the birth. She had barely had time to get used to her new surroundings before her lord was brought home on a rail, his neck broken in a point to point. She continued to live quietly, her oldest sister coming to be with her for her confinement, and when Ellen found out she had had a daughter, her first thought was one of gratitude that the Marquess was not there to know. He had never considered the possibility that the child would be anything but his heir. How angry he would have been, she thought, with this small, screaming, red-faced, red-haired female!

Lord Winship's heir was a second cousin, one William Winship, who had reluctantly given up all hopes of succeeding to the title after the Marquess's marriage. His expectations were raised again at the untimely death of Lord Winship, but when he attended the funeral and saw Ellen's pregnancy, he was much cast down. When Mary Ellen was born however, he lost no time in presenting himself at Braxton with his wife, Hortensia. The new Marchioness of Braxton took one look at the beautiful widow, just eighteen, and started her campaign to remove her from the vicinity immediately. She knew William was very much under the cat's foot, but even he could not fail to compare his plain, rail-thin wife with this tempting blond beauty. And men were apt to be so silly, as her mother had warned her time and time again.

Somehow, Ellen found herself packing to join her brother in Scotland instead of moving into the very pleasant dower house on the estate. For one thing, outside of her marriage settlement, the Marquess had not made any provision for her in his will, thinking that, at the age of only thirty-eight, he had many more years left to him before he stuck his spoon in the wall. From luxury to genteel poverty was a quick step for Lady Winship, but she might have been able to stay in England and see her sisters and friends if Hortensia had not found her husband kissing her hand so fervently and attempting to take her in his arms, one day in the conservatory.

When that lady frigidly suggested she might be more comfortable with her own family, and pledged her such a generous allowance as well, what was the young dowager-marchioness to do? She had the vague feeling that she had been at fault in not controlling the new heir's ardor, and since Hortensia encouraged this interpretation, she was glad to accept the lady's offer and take herself and her baby off. However, she was wiser at thirty-five than she had been at eighteen, and she was determined that at least Mariel should have her chance before she buried herself here in the hills. She wanted her to enjoy some pretty clothes and festive parties; to learn to flirt with handsome young men and break some hearts in passing; to see the sights in town and go to the theater and the opera; to wonder which of four invitations for one evening she wished to accept; to be showered with bouquets and compliments and attention! In short, she wanted her to have fun! How she was to get her daughter to agree to this plan she had no idea, and she shook her head sadly as she picked up a pair of James's heavy wool socks that needed darning and threaded her needle.

Out in the yard, Mariel took a deep breath of the cool, rainy air and smiled happily. She had to walk fast to keep up with her uncle, and in order to slow him down a bit, she reached for his hand as she used to do when she was little.

"Uncle! Is there any special reason for such haste this morning? You haven't had any bad news from the shepherds, have you?"

Her uncle gave her his brief and seldom seen smile. "Nay, Mariel, but I am anxious about two of the new ewes. Rorry mentioned last night that he didn't like the way they were carrying on." He opened the gate to the field and pushed through, in a hurry to reach the sheep and see for himself that his beloved flock had come through the night safely. James MacDonald was a good farmer, but he knew that even with the best care and provision being made, there were always fatalities at lambing time. The sheepcot seemed warm after the windswept field, and Mariel rubbed her hands together gratefully while her uncle inspected the ewes. Rorry grinned at her briefly before he began a deeply technical discussion with his employer. To a more gently bred girl the scene would have been horrifying. The blood, the newborn lambs and straining ewes making a great din in the small space might have caused most young ladies to gasp and faint, but Mariel was used to it. She inspected the new additions to the flock as carefully as her uncle did, and was perfectly content to sit on a bale of hay until he finished his business with his head shepherd. Mariel was not sentimental about sheep, but she had to admit that the newborn lambs were very appealing, so small and dear, and she hoped the cold rain would stop soon for their sakes. They were at their most vulnerable in the first hours of their lives, and a sudden drop in temperature could mean the difference between success or failure in expanding the flock for that season.

Eventually James was satisfied, and went on with his niece to the barns. It was early afternoon before he headed back to the hall, Mariel still at his side. Her cheeks were rosy now from the cold, damp air, and what hair had escaped from her shawl was misted with moisture and curling wildly. She pushed it back impatiently, knowing she would be sent to her room to brush it in order as soon as her mother saw her. That reminded her of the conversation at the breakfast table, and she chuckled. Her uncle looked down at her inquiringly, one eyebrow raised, and she said, "I was just remembering this morning, and mother's silly scheme to take me to London! I do hope she will come to agree with me that such a plan is absurd! I have no desire for it at all!"

James frowned a little and paused, weighing his words before he spoke. "Aye lass, *you* have no desire for it!"

"Whatever do you mean, uncle? Surely it was for my sake that mother proposed it!"

"Aye, 'tis true she wants you to have a better chance in life than she has had. I agree with her that you should see more of the world than just these mountains, fields, and loch." He looked around him contentedly as he spoke, and Mariel laughed.

"Oh uncle, you are so happy here! *You* don't want to see the world! Why should I?"

Her uncle took her hand gently and looked down into her bright face. "'Tis never good to decide where you want to spend your life until you have something to compare it to. You should see England, and perhaps Europe too before you come home to Scotland, if so you choose. I traveled there myself, you know."

Mariel was shocked for she had been sure her uncle would applaud her sentiments and help her convince her mother to give up the scheme. James began walking again and she hurried to keep up with him, deep in thought. They were almost to the door of the hall when she said suddenly, "But uncle, you said *I* have no desire for it. Do you mean *mother* does?"

He sighed and tried to explain. "Look my girl, your mother was wed when she was but your age, and widowed even before you were born! She never went to London for a season—outside of her wedding journey she never went anywhere, for Lord Winship wed her right from the schoolroom. Is it any wonder she misses the gaiety she has never had? Of course the trip is for you, but it would also give her a chance to see London and meet her sisters and friends again. She has lived here for seventeen years in only our company, saving her money so you could have this opportunity. Perhaps Mariel . . ." he paused and scowled before he continued, "perhaps in denying her the treat, you are being selfish?"

His niece looked at him wonderingly as he opened the door to the hall and ushered her in. After they had hung up their wet coats, he went away to the estate room, leaving her to ponder his last words. The hall was empty and she sat down by the fire to think.

Was her mother lonely, with only her brother and her child to bear her company for so much of the year? She had never said so, or acted as if her life were boring and confining. But then, Mariel admitted honestly to herself, because I was so happy, I never considered my mother's feelings. And I suppose it is possible, she added fairly without understanding the sentiment in the least, to not like farms and solitude, and wild wintry weather that keeps you indoors for weeks at a time, and the autumn rains that sometimes seem as if they will never stop. She remembered that her mother was not an ardent horsewoman either, so she seldom went for a ride as Mariel did with such regularity, and she never joined Uncle James to inspect the fields or the flock. Mariel had thought her mother perfectly content to oversee the house and work on her needlepoint and read the books she had delivered from town whenever she had the chance.

I wonder what it was like to be married at seventeen, she thought. I wonder if my mother loved my father and her life at Braxton Hall? And imagine losing your husband before you were married a year! It must have been a frightening experience to be so young and alone, and to know that you were going to have a baby as well! Mariel had not known her MacDonald grandparents, but from things her uncle and her mother had let slip, she had been sure they were dour, serious people. Why else would James have left his home when he inherited this farm from his uncle Edward, and why would her mother come here if her own parents were loving and sympathetic? If she had not wanted to live on at Braxton in the dower house, she could have returned to her parents, but she had not. Mariel realized that she had never thought to question her mother's decision, and that in fact she knew very little about her and what she missed in her life. She was "mother"; not a person in her own right. Mariel shook her head and wandered up the stairs to change her damp dress, thinking that perhaps she had been more selfish than she knew.

When she came back downstairs, her hair dry and neatly brushed, she found her mother busy in the still room with one of the maids. Before she could even think of a question, she was put to work, and somehow it was impossible to ask what she wanted to know with Fiona there, chattering away as she always did. Fiona had been with them for ten years and considered herself part of the family, as so she was. A distant relative of the clan MacDonald, she was a good worker even if her tongue did wag on both ends at once, as Uncle James claimed. Mariel and her mother exchanged a smile over the little maid's head.

At dinner, the talk was all of the lambing, and a trip to Dundee on the morrow that Lady Winship planned to make if the weather cleared. Mariel was sent to the piano after dinner while her mother and uncle sat on either side of the fire, conversing softly and taking notice of her only when she struck a wrong note or mistimed a measure. Mariel enjoyed the piano and loved to sing, but this evening she had no desire for it, and soon began to play a melancholy air she had heard from a wandering minstrel at the last harvest fair. As she played, she pondered again what her uncle had said. How could anyone, she wondered, wish to leave Lochcrae Farm? And if she agreed to go, how could she bear to be away from it for such a long time? She had no idea how long a period comprised a season, but somehow she knew it was not the matter of a few short weeks! And she would miss the best part of the year; the spring and summer with the smell of heather and new-mown hay in the fields, and all the bright blue days when the loch was so calm it looked like a sheet of green glass! And she would not be here in the cool mornings when the mist hid the mountain tops and she could rise early as she often did for a solitary ride down the dewy lanes.

She sighed, and rose from the piano, closing it softly, and then she went to sit on a small footstool at her uncle's feet and stared into the flames while he ruffled her hair gently.

"Such a sad song, my dear!" her mother teased. "No wonder you have decided to stop! Do you go with me to Dundee tomorrow or would you prefer to stay with your uncle? If I cannot find the material I want, James," she added to her brother, "I may remain another day."

"I will come with you, Mama!" Mariel said quickly, although she would have preferred to stay on the farm. When she saw her mother's face light up in pleasure, she was glad she had given in to the generous impulse, and went away to bed more happily.

The following morning was bright and clear, all trace of the rain gone, leaving the world looking fresh-washed and sparkling. Lady Winship took the reins of the pony trap gaily and flourished her whip at her brother, standing on the shallow front steps of the hall to see them off.

"You may not see us until tomorrow, James!" she said with a smile. Mariel took her seat beside her, dressed in her best navy wool gown with its matching cape thrown over her shoulders. She hoped they could finish their shopping today and be home in time for dinner. As they drove away at a fast trot, Mariel took a deep breath and asked, "Mother, are you ever lonesome, here at Lochcrae?"

Her mother turned sideways a little, startled by the question.

"Lonesome? Who could be lonesome with such a hubbub as you and your uncle make all the time?" Suddenly she dropped her bantering air and replied seriously, "Well, yes, Mariel, sometimes I am lonesome when you are busy with your uncle, or when the weather is bad and I cannot get out to attend church." She looked at her daughter seriously. "You must not think that I am unhappy, my dear. I have you and my dear brother after all, and all the activity that makes up my days. Indeed, sometimes I wonder how I am ever to finish, I am so busy!"

She laughed, but she was watching her daughter carefully, wondering what had prompted the question.

"I mean," Mariel said with a frown on her face, "do you ever miss Braxton Hall and all the parties and amusements you were used to?"

Her mother laughed again gently. "I was not used to any such 'amusements' as you describe. You forget I was with child when I returned from my wedding journey, and we lived very quietly awaiting your birth. Your father..." she paused, and now it was her turn to frown, "your father did not care for levity or parties. He was... he was a very serious man."

Mariel considered this awful statement. She had known her mother to be a gay and happy person all her life. Surely at age seventeen it must have been difficult to sit serenely uncomplaining with a "serious" man.

"How did you meet my father?" she asked eagerly. Perhaps there was a romance here such as she had read about, and if you were very much in love, it would not matter if there were no friends or parties to attend, for you would want to be alone with the man you loved.

Lady Winship touched the pony's broad back gently with her whip before she replied. "He came to visit my father for the hunting, and before I knew it had asked for my hand."

"Were you pleased, Mother? Did you love him?" Mariel asked shyly. Her mother took a moment before she answered.

"I did not know him very well, dear. I thought he

was merely a friend of my father's, so his proposal was a complete surprise. My mother and father considered it an excellent match, even if he was so much older than I."

Mariel had never realized that perhaps her mother had not gone into marriage wholeheartedly, and she framed her next question carefully.

"How much older was he, Mother?"

"He was thirty-eight to my seventeen. I do not want you to think I was not happy, Mariel; your father was everything that was kind, and I was sorry later I had made such a fuss..."

Her voice died away, as if she felt she had said too much.

"Made a fuss, Mother? Why? Oh, you didn't want to, did you? Mother, were you *forced* to marry him?"

Her mother stared straight ahead at the country lane before them, her face pale. "There was no such thing as setting up your will against your parents in those days, Mariel. My father decided I should marry him, and although I tried to protest, it was no use. But we were content, the little time we had together. I would not wish it so for you, my dear," she added, turning to smile at her horrified daughter. "When the time comes, I would wish you to love the man who asks for your hand, and I would never try to coerce you into a loveless match, no matter how advantageous! I do hope, however, that you will fall in love with someone suitable!"

Mariel tried to laugh, her mind still running over the truly shocking things she had just heard. "There is plenty of time before we have to consider that!" she said, and her mother agreed with her usual calm composure.

As they were then entering the village, they were soon busy nodding and smiling to their neighbors and the vicar who passed them in his gig. When they again reached the open road, the subject was not reopened, and they chatted of other things.

In Dundee, they left the pony and trap at the inn Lady Winship always patronized, and arranged for rooms in case they were forced to remain overnight. After a brief luncheon in their private parlor where the landlady regaled Lady Winship with all the town gossip, they gathered their reticules and cloaks and began their shopping. Mariel soon found herself burdened with all manner of bundles and parcels and hoped her mother would have the drapery material she was even then selecting sent to the inn.

At last Lady Winship declared herself satisfied. As they began to retrace their steps to the inn, she came to an abrupt stop before the windows of a milliner's shop.

"Oh look, Mariel!" she cried. "Isn't it beautiful?"

Mariel inspected the bonnet that had caught her mother's eye carefully. It had a high peaked crown of soft green straw and was wrapped around with matching veiling of a delicate shade of green, interspersed with tiny white flowers. Mariel realized it would be most becoming to her mother and persuaded her to try it on.

"But I was thinking of you, love!" she protested as Mariel propelled her firmly into the shop.

"Nonsense, Mother! You know that is *your* hat!"

The milliner was delighted to assist them, and Lady Winship sighed as the confection was carefully lowered onto her gleaming blond curls. Mariel thought she had never seen her mother look so becoming. *Why, she realized with a shock, she is not old at all, and she looks beautiful in that bonnet!*

The milliner agreed with her fervently, exclaiming over the lady's lovely eyes, but Lady Winship removed the bonnet firmly. "'Tis fetching, I agree, but I have no use for such frippery! Come, Mariel, we must be going!"

She drew on her gloves and had started to pick up her parcels when Mariel said impulsively, "But Mother, surely in London you will need a smart bonnet! You cannot mean to wear the old black straw you wear to kirk when you are in town!"

Lady Winship dropped her parcels. "In London?" she asked faintly. "But... but..."

"In London," Mariel said firmly. "When we are there for the season, of course!"

Her mother hugged her. "Oh Mariel, do you mean it? You *do* want to go? Oh my dear, 'tis the wish of my heart come true!"

Mariel assured her that she was serious, and Lady Winship, glowing with happiness, purchased the bonnet and insisted on carrying the bandbox back to the inn herself.

She talked continuously as they walked along.

"Now we must stay in Dundee tonight, my love, for we have a vast amount of shopping to do! Not that we shall buy everything here, oh no! When we reach London we shall visit all the finest modistes, for you must not be seen in anything provincial you know. That would be fatal!"

Mariel was glad her mother was so occupied with her plans, for her own heart sank when she considered to what she had committed herself. As her mother rambled on about dimities and silks and laces and the impossibility of finding a local dressmaker who could produce anything of the first consequence, and how busy she was going to be in the weeks that followed, and how she had to write to Lady Daphne Carleton, her dear aunt who had so often begged her to come and make a long stay with her, Mariel's mind saw only the green spring fields of Lochcrae, and the white gulls, crying over the loch, and she felt a great sadness.

When they reached their rooms at the inn however, she could only be glad she had agreed when she saw the happiness in her mother's face. A season was not forever, she told herself staunchly, and in a few months she would be back in Lochcrae and never, never have to leave it again! She sat down to tea much more cheerfully, and attended to her mother's plans for the morrow with no hint of sacrifice on her face.

TWO

In the days that followed, Mariel tried hard to be as enthusiastic about the coming trip to London as her mother was. She knew her uncle was pleased with her decision, and she tried to forget that she might be with him overseeing the farm instead of sitting demurely in the morning room sewing a new lace collar to one of her second-best dresses. She did not have to forego everything of course; he often took her away to see the new lambs, or for a ride to the village or the loch, and her mother, knowing how hard the coming separation would be, always agreed that she should go.

Lady Winship had written immediately to her aunt, Lady Carleton, and anxiously waited her reply. It was some three weeks later when the letter finally arrived. Of course her dear Ellen and her lovely daughter Mariel—such a cunning name, she quite longed to see her—

must stay with her for the season. She and Algernon were becoming a dull older couple she declared, now that their daughters were both married, and they saw so little of dear Algy, their only son. She seemed a bit tart on this point, declaring that the young man's friends had first priority, and all his activities—heavily underlined—kept him so busy. But now, with dear Ellen to bear her company, and a pretty young girl to present to society, her spirits were quite revived. She begged them to set forth on the journey as soon as possible, for she was all impatience for their arrival.

Lady Winship smiled as she read the letter again and again.

"You will like Daphne, my dear," she confided to Mariel. "I mean Lady Carleton, of course! She was my mother's youngest sister, so much younger that she seemed more like an older friend than an aunt to me, and she was very kind to me when I was a little girl. Whenever she visited there was sure to be fun and laughter and jokes. How Daphne loved a good joke! Sometimes it was hard to remember she was Mama's sister, so unlike as they were! When I married, oh, long after her to be sure, she wrote and begged me to visit her so many times. To think we have not seen each other for seventeen years!" Lady Winship sighed and read the letter once again.

Uncle James arranged for them to travel by coastal packet from Edinburgh to London. The journey by land was tiresomely long, even in a private carriage, and in spite of Mr. MacAdam's new road surface in many places, and Thomas Telford's new bridges and canals. Both men, he proudly pointed out, were Scots of course!

There was also the inconvenience of putting up each night at the inns along the way, not all of them suited to a lady's nice tastes with their coarse food and damp unaired sheets. He wished he might go with them and escort them safely, but he could not leave the farm for so long a period. If, however, they went by the packet which he would carefully select, they would be far more comfortable, and if the winds were right, arrive in town much sooner than would have been possible plodding along behind a team day after day.

He spent many hours with Lady Winship going over finances and plans, while Mariel wandered around the farm and tried to memorize her favorite spots against the long separation. James insisted his sister take a large draft on his London bank, and when she would have demurred, saying she had saved a long time for this trip, he would not listen.

"Hush now, Ellen! I know you think you are well before with the world, but the extra money will allow you to do everything in the first style of elegance! Let it be my gift to you and Mariel, for I shall like to think of you setting out for a ball, dressed finer than any of the others."

Lady Winship finally agreed and kissed her brother warmly, tears in her eyes. James hugged her gruffly, and made a quick escape before the sparkling drops began to fall.

He also made a special point of taking Mariel aside one day and talking to her seriously about what she could expect in town, and how she should comport herself as a debutante. When she laughed at his lecture he shook his finger at her sternly and said, "Aye, lass, 'tis all a game I know! But I also know *you,* Mary Ellen Winship, and you have been falling into scrapes since you first began to toddle! London is no place for your mad-brained escapades and ill-judged starts!"

Mariel would have protested, but he added, "Don't you think I know who hid the Vicar's gig behind the ale shop in the village, or who went fishing on the loch last summer with Robby and Geordie Knox when she should have been fast asleep in bed? Gie o'er! 'Tis your Uncle James, not your mother speaking to you, and I say you shall behave!"

So awed by his knowledge of what she had considered successfully unknown frolics, Mariel could only nod her head meekly.

It seemed no time at all before the last gowns were delivered from Dundee, the trunks and bandboxes packed, and the day of departure arrived. James was to drive them to Edinburgh, a journey of a long two days, and he insisted on an early start. The morning was overcast and chilly, and Mariel wrapped her new cloak around her more closely as she stood for a moment by the carriage door and stared back up at the hall. The Dugans were waving from the door, and Fiona was chattering away and trying not to cry with the other maids, while some of the farm hands secured the baggage to the boot. Mariel felt a big lump in her throat, and her eyes blurred as she took a last long look at the only home she had ever known and had so dearly loved. She might have cried then, except she heard her mother's happy laugh as she waved good-bye to the servants, and that stiffened her back and helped her dry her eyes. She was committed and there was no turning back; well, she would go with grace and never let her mother know how sad it made her to leave Lochcrae.

Mariel had never visited Edinburgh, and as they drove into the city late the following day, exclaimed over its size. Lady Winship was sure that London must be far larger and grander, but James declared Edinburgh a bonny place, much improved from its earlier condition. As they wended their way through the busy streets, he told her how the town fathers had decreed a new city, and how it had been steadily built in the last generation. They all agreed it was indeed a capital of art and intellect, and beautiful buildings and bridges. Lady Winship wished they might have time to visit the birthplace of Walter Scott, one of her favorite authors, and one who had done so much to educate the English to the fact that this northern domain was not just a land of Celtic savages as they had so long believed. Unfortunately James maintained it was too late for sightseeing since they had to board the packet at dawn.

Mariel was glad it was not raining the next morning for that would have been too hard to bear. Her uncle saw their luggage safely aboard the packet and stowed in their cabin, while Mariel remained on deck to say good-bye when he returned from below. When he saw her unhappy expression, he took her in his arms and said gruffly, "Aye, I know, lass, I know, but you're a good girl and it won't be forever! Enjoy yourself, learn what you can, and be a credit to us!"

Mariel tried to speak but she could not, so she just hugged him hard and nodded her head. Her mother wept a little until James declared he had had quite enough and he would never have agreed to the scheme if he had known it was going to turn his family into a pair of watering pots! All too soon he was striding away, his black beard blowing in the wind.

Lady Winship wiped her eyes and eyed the slatting sails a little dubiously before saying in a hopeful voice, "A strong breeze will have us in London in no time, my dear! Do come below and see the cubby that is our cabin! 'Tis just as well it will be a short journey, for how we are to live so confined I do not know!"

After inspecting the cabin, Mariel had to agree with her, and was glad to escape back to the deck when they made sail and headed out of the Firth of Forth towards the North Sea. She wondered if she were going to be seasick when the packet plunged into the first of the heavy swells, but to her surprise, both she and her mother were fine. Mrs. Leslie, whom they had met while at anchor and who had promised to be a pleasant traveling companion, was not seen again until they reached the calm waters past Canvey Island and the approach to London.

Mariel found the whole voyage fascinating—the sailors trimming sails, the smell of the salt air and the movements of the packet as she buried her forefoot in the waves and beat her way to London, and the sunsets over England when even the gulls were quiet and peaceful. Mariel was astounded that when she finally set foot on land again at Woolwich, it seemed as if she were still at sea, and she and her mother clutched each other and laughed as they staggered slightly, their hard-won sea legs now a hindrance.

Lady Carleton and her husband were there to meet them, and one look at that lady's beaming round face and stout comfortable figure did much to reassure Mariel of their welcome. Lord Carleton was as tall and thin as his wife was short and fat, and appeared to be a man of very few words. Of course, Mariel decided, that might be because his wife never stopped talking! She had embraced Lady Winship fervently, tipping her elaborate bonnet over one eye as she did so, and exclaiming, "My dear Ellen!—would have known you anywhere!—not really fair, you know—so lovely still—buried in Scotland—Algernon, do see!—and where is your daughter?—oh, Mariel, of course, there you are—mother's eyes, that's a good thing!—the carriage, Algernon! Are we to stand here all day in this crush of people?—Ellen, cream of cucumber, I think—freckles are not *in* this season!"

Lord Carleton did not try to answer as he turned and beckoned to the two footmen standing near an elaborate town carriage. Without making any sort of fuss, or giving more than a few terse orders, he soon had the smaller bags stowed and arrangements made to transfer their trunks to his home in St. James Square, and was handing them up into the carriage.

Mariel sat close to the window; she wanted to see everything she could of this new world she found herself in. The busy waterfront, the drays going back and forth loaded with cargo and provisions, the ships tied up, hundreds of them it seemed, were all fascinating. Even the smell of the tarry ropes and the spice warehouses seemed exhilarating, and she was glad Lady Carleton continued to talk nonstop to her mother so she could drink it all in uninterrupted.

They were soon away, proceeding to town at a brisk pace. At first, Mariel was disappointed, for London seemed to be a collection of small villages and nowhere near as impressive as Edinburgh, but before long they were in the city streets and moving very slowly because of the crowds of people and vehicles in their path. Mariel stared silently at the tall, narrow tenements and teeming alleys. The smell was unbelievable; she wondered how anyone could endure it! Even as she watched, a window was thrown open and a pail of slops emptied on the unwary passersby below.

Lady Carleton was still chattering away, forcibly reminding Mariel of Fiona, but now she paused for a moment to search in her capacious reticule until she found a large handkerchief scented with lavender water which she handed to Mariel. Mariel took it gratefully and buried her nose in it as Lord Carleton said kindly, "Soon be better! Not far now!"

At last they drew away from the poorer, more crowded sections, and she was able once again to pay attention to the beautiful buildings and parks that they passed. Lord Carleton occasionally pointed out the window of the coach and said briefly, "Pall Mall!" or "Westminster!", but Mariel was completely confused, and the thought of never being allowed out without a footman or a maid in attendance was much more acceptable than it had been when her mother first told her of its necessity. At least, being Londoners, they would know their way home!

Lord and Lady Carleton's town house was most impressive, situated as it was in St. James Square, so handy to the gentlemen's clubs, as well as to Pall Mall and St. James Park and as Lady Carleton pointed out, "Right in the heart of all the social world!" Mariel tried hard not to stare at the impressive butler who bowed them into the front hall. He was even taller and more dignified than Lord Carleton!

"Ah, Ridgeway, there you are!" Lady Carleton exclaimed with every indication of delight, although where Ridgeway might have been other than at his accustomed post was not explained. He bowed austerely as he was introduced to Lady Winship and Mariel, but he did not deign to smile.

Lord Carleton disappeared, his duty done, not that his wife noticed his absence in the slightest as she continued to talk to her guests.

"Now, Ellen my dear,—Mariel too, of course,—do you want to rest?—wash the travel dirt away?—or, oh dear, you cannot do that! I am longing to hear all about your journey, and Scotland too, of course,—and besides, Algernon is coming to tea!"

She beamed happily, and Mariel wondered if her husband was in the habit of neglecting her until she rambled on, "My son, you know! Such a dear boy! So busy! But word of a Carleton, he promised! I am so anxious that he meet Mariel!"

She turned and took both Mariel's hands in hers and said earnestly, "It is so much pleasanter, my dear, when you have someone you know, to show you how to go on, and give you the hint about what society demands, and what you must on no account do! Naturally, Algy is awake on every suit!"

Bustling forward after a final squeeze and a loving smile, she took Lady Winship's arm and led the way to the drawing room. Mariel handed her cloak to the butler and followed, letting out a gasp as she crossed the threshold, a sound that did not escape her hostess.

"It *is* something like, isn't it?" she asked proudly. "I have faithfully followed all the Prince Regent's dictates on design, and feel it is such a success that even Prinny himself might feel at home here—if ever he were to come, I mean!"

Mariel stared at the Chinese vases, side by side with crocodile-legged tables, the massive chandeliers, the sofas and chairs and footstools and urns, and more elaborate bric-a-brac on every available surface than she had ever seen. The windows were draped in heavy red velvet, much adorned with tassels and gold braid, and a hot fire burned in the massive fireplace.

"It is quite unusual, ma'am!" Mariel got out, as her mother smiled and nodded at her.

Lady Carleton begged them to be seated by the fire, and the two older ladies were soon deep in conversation again, with Mariel adding a few words whenever directly addressed. She thought Lady Carleton a love, in spite of her nonstop chatter and disjointed sentences, and when she told of her latest misadventure,—"would you believe, my dears, lost one of my slippers—right on Bond Street—and of course Countess Esterhazy had to see it—so funny!"—both Winships had to laugh with her.

In the meantime, Algernon Carleton was getting ready to walk from his rooms on Whitcomb Street to join his mother for tea. He frowned at his reflection in the mirror over the mantel and altered one fold of his cravat slightly.

"Do you think I've overdone it?" he asked earnestly of the other young man present who was lounging back in an easy chair by the side of the fireplace. "Perhaps I should have left it as it was...."

"My dear Algy," the other gentleman said with a yawn, "since you ask my opinion, I think you *always* overdo it!"

Mr. Carleton did not appear to be offended by this blunt appraisal of his sartorial splendor. "The trouble with you, John, is that you have no sense of style! Just look at this coat! Had it made at Stulz's, y'know! Only one like it in London!"

"Thank heavens!" his incorrigible friend said fervently. "Although come to think of it, who else would want such a thing?"

"Here now, John, what can you mean? Look at the lapels, the set of the shoulders..."

"I would be glad to do so, if I could get past the color! Why lavender, Algy? Why?" He shuddered, and folding the newspaper he had been reading, rose and stretched. "It certainly is unique, if that's what you were striving for! And if I may say so, I would not have chosen bisque pantaloons to complete the ensemble!"

The Honorable Mr. Carleton ignored him. "Know what it is, John?" he asked as he picked up his gloves and a clouded cane. "You're jealous, that's all! Wish you'd thought of it yourself! At least you must admit the cravat is perfect, and I only had to discard a mere dozen before I got it right!"

His friend surveyed the flowing white neckpiece so carefully arranged between towering shirt points.

"I hope you can swallow, dear boy, if you are going to tea!"

"Of course I can swallow!" Mr. Carleton said indignantly. "You are obviously stunned by its originality!

33

'Tis one of my own creations. I call it the Carleton Cascade! Apt, eh?"

John laughed as he accompanied his friend to the door. He was not so tall as Algernon Carleton, and attired as he was in dark brown with only a single signet ring as adornment, he tended to recede into the background in comparison. Besides the lavender coat and bisque pantaloons, Algernon sported several fobs and rings and an ornate quizzing glass as well as the clouded cane. He was much thinner than John, and seemed younger with his rosy complexion, butter-yellow hair, and bright blue eyes. At twenty-three he enjoyed life to the fullest and was always ready for whatever fun or frolic was afoot, and he had many friends who considered him the best of chaps in spite of his regrettable tendency towards dandyism. John Greeton was a year older with broad shoulders and powerful legs and hands that looked as if they had done their share of work. His face was so tanned that his smile appeared startlingly white in comparison. Of the two, he was the more handsome with strong features and dark brows, set over a pair of intelligent hazel eyes. He was new come from the country for the season and was accepted everywhere for his good manners and sunny good nature, as well as his wry turn of phrase, although he was quieter than the other young blades.

The two strolled together to Carleton House, enjoying the spring sunshine and chatting easily.

"I assume you attend your mother in response to a direct invitation?" John asked idly. "I find it hard to believe you are going to waste such splendor on a family tea party on your own initiative!"

"To be honest, John, it was more an order than an invitation! Might have refused, but m'father reinforced the plan, and since I am quite done up at the moment, thought it best to agree! Don't plan to enjoy it though!

Mother has invited her niece Lady Winship and her daughter to stay with her during the season. They have been buried in Scotland forever! Sure to be ghastly! With my luck the girl will probably be fat and dowdy with a terrible accent and I will be expected to do the pretty on every occasion! I cannot bear to think of it!"

His friend interrupted these melancholy thoughts. "But think of the pleasure you are giving her, my boy. Such style, such splendor! She is sure to be especially struck by the lavender coat! How kind of you to give her such a treat!"

Algernon grinned. "None of your sauce, John! Do you go to Wheatons' tonight? Lord Bristow invited me to join his party for cards but I was forced to refuse because of the Wheatons' previous invitation. Wish I'd known there was a game afoot—a reception ain't in it with that!"

John admitted he was promised to Lord Bristow as the two reached the steps of Carleton House. After they arranged to ride the following afternoon, they parted, John to continue on to his club, and Algernon to bound up the shallow steps and enter the house.

He refused to be announced, tossing his hat gaily to a disapproving Ridgeway, who sniffed as the young man knocked lightly on the drawing-room door and immediately entered.

Algernon braced himself for a moment on the threshold and then moved forward to where his mother sat smiling and beckoning to him. He bowed gracefully as she exclaimed, "Dear Algy! So good of you! You must let me make you known to my niece Lady Winship and her daughter Mariel."

Her son turned politely to the lady seated beside his mother and his mouth dropped open. What glorious vision was this, and how had anything so perfect come to adorn that quite ordinary sofa, now honored forever because she had chosen to sit on it? Lady Winship gave him her hand and he bowed over it reverently.

"Servant, ma'am! Most obedient servant!" he breathed.

Lady Winship smiled at him, causing his heart to miss a beat. Such a beautiful smile, such perfect teeth along with that delicate complexion, and those light green eyes, sparkling with amusement, all combined to strike him dumb. On the other side of the fireplace, Mariel watched in amazement. She was forcibly reminded of an Easter egg, although Mr. Carleton was not the right shape, and she tried hard to control her expression so he might not guess how absurd she found him. Lady Carleton beamed at him again and said, "And here is little Mariel!"

Reluctantly, he dropped Lady Winship's hand and turned around to see a pert little miss with a mop of red hair and good heavens!—freckles, surveying him seriously.

"How do you do?" he asked, wondering if his mama could do anything with her before he was forced to escort her around town.

Mariel grinned at him. "Very well, I thank you, er... but how do we address each other, sir? We are in some way related if my mother is your mother's niece, but are we cousins?"

Lady Carleton intervened. "Sit down, Algy, do! We will break our necks peering up at you! Mariel, you are of course my great-niece—good heavens, really don't feel old enough for that—but Algy and your mother are cousins, so that makes you Algy's second cousin?—a great cousin?—doesn't sound right!—a cousin once removed? Tch!" She subsided, still thinking, while Algy got right to the heart of the matter.

"Dear cousin Ellen! I cannot tell you how delightful

it is to welcome you! And, of course, your daughter too!" he added hastily.

At that moment there was a discreet knock on the door, and Ridgeway entered followed by two footmen with the tea tray. Lady Carleton was recalled to her surroundings when Ridgeway handed her a cup, and the footmen passed around small plates of cake. Algy turned his attention away from the goddess seated across from him and reluctantly addressed Mariel again.

"Are you thrilled to be in town, Lady Mariel? Must be devilish boring, being buried in the wilds of Scotland!"

Mariel looked at him sternly, her green eyes flashing fire.

"Not at all, sir! Scotland is exceedingly salubrious; in fact the city of Edinburgh does not have to bow to London in any way. Surely there are not the slums and smells that I found today in *that* city's streets! Besides, I have never been bored there!"

Lady Winship broke in in her gentle musical voice.

"Of course Mariel is delighted, as I am myself, to be here for the season, cousin. And it is so good of your mother to invite us to stay!" She smiled at Lady Carleton, still lost in thought as she tried to untangle cousins and nephews and aunts. Ah, Algy thought, what a lovely voice, so soft and melodious! She is an angel!

"I hope you will allow me to escort you, cousin Ellen," he breathed fervently, and when the lady said she would be delighted to have his company for herself and her daughter, his cup ran over with joy.

Mariel for her part was stunned. Could it be that this ridiculous creature had conceived a *tendre* for mama? Didn't he see what a cake he was making of himself? He could not be a day over twenty-five, and Mama was all of ten years older than that! And that silly coat and ostentatious cravat and the points on his shirt collar reaching half way up his cheeks and making it impossible for him to turn his head easily—how absurd! Oh, how she wished Uncle James could see him!

Lady Carleton shook off her abstraction and begged Mariel to have another macaroon, or perhaps some more lady fingers, and Algy was free to drink in the marvelous creature seated across from him. Lady Winship sat quietly, sipping her tea and staring into the fire. She was a little tired from the bustle of packing and landing, and the ride from Woolwich, and she hoped it would not be much longer before Daphne showed them to their rooms so she might rest. She did not seem aware of the reverent attention of her cousin Algy, for she had quickly classified him as a young man who aspired to dandyism, and she could only hope for his sake that he would outgrow the tendency as he matured. She had known immediately that Mariel would take him in dislike, and hoped there were other young men in London who were not so foppish, but she would be glad to rely on his escort until she had more friends to call on. He was, after all, Lord Carleton's son, and he and Mariel were bound to be thrown into each other's company a great deal. What a pity that he was so full of affectation!

The tea party was drawing to a close when Lord Carleton appeared. He stood in the doorway, his brows raised as he surveyed his son, and then he lifted his quizzing glass for a closer inspection. That look had all too often embarrassed Algy, but this afternoon he was completely unaware of it, and did not even know his father was in the room until that gentleman wandered over and said gently,

"Lavender, Algy? My, my! I beg the indulgence of a moment before you leave."

His son quickly rose and bowed as Lady Carleton gathered up her reticule and handkerchief and prepared to take her guests away to rest before dinner. Algy was desperately trying to think of a way to escape the Wheatons' reception so he might inveigle an invitation to dinner when the ladies left the drawing room. His mother mentioned in passing that she would be obliged if he could arrange to escort them to the theater the following evening, and he hastened to agree. Since his mother began to talk quickly to the Winships of the play they were to see, she missed the significance of such ready acquiescence from one she too often had to coax and cajole if she wanted his attendance. Lord Carleton poured himself a glass of wine and waited until Algy had bowed the ladies out. Breathing a fervent "'Til tomorrow!" to the divine Ellen, he rejoined his father, now seated by the fire.

"A glass of wine, my boy?" that gentleman asked. "I cannot tell you how gratified I am that your busy schedule permits you to attend me!"

Ordinarily Algy would have been alarmed and beaten a hasty retreat, but now he was so bemused he merely poured the wine and took his seat again.

"It has come to my attention," his father began, "that you have been dipping mighty deep these last few weeks. Heard from Viscount Sterling that you lost a great deal of money at Whites on Tuesday last. I hope you know what you are about! I think it only fair to warn you, I have no intention of bailing you out of debt yet once again!"

At these ominous words, Algy came out of his reverie and stared at his father's stern face.

"Not to worry, sir, not to worry!" he said airily. "I'll soon come about! Never saw the cards to run so much against me, but another few nights should see me straight again!"

His father shuddered and set down his glass. "Have you ever considered, Algy, that your best course might be to forego cards? And horse racing and prize fights? And, oh yes, ridiculous wagers such as how many ladies carrying pink parasols would pass a certain street corner in fifteen minutes? I heard you dropped fifty guineas on that!"

Algy flushed a little and said defensively, "Almost had it won, sir, 'pon my word! If only the last one hadn't favored green! Terrible taste!"

His father rose and strolled to the door, saying over his shoulder, "How unfortunate! Do remember what I have said, however. You are on your own till next quarter day, and I should so dislike hearing my son had been taken up for bad debts. Newgate can hardly be called good ton, my boy!"

On these comforting words he waved gently and left the room, leaving Algy no alternative but to recover his cane and hat from Ridgeway and make his way home.

THREE

Upstairs, in the spacious bedroom Lady Carleton had indicated was to be hers, Mariel was making the acquaintance of her new maid. She was a very young maid, thrilled to be elevated to the post of abigail, and determined to do her best for her new mistress. It was not long before both girls were chatting easily as they unpacked. When Mariel learned that Annie was from a farm in Ireland, she was sure they would deal famously together, and was soon telling her all about Lochcrae and her Uncle James. Making her way down the back stairs with Lady Mariel's evening gown to press for dinner, Annie shook her head a little. If she had the chance to come to town, wear beautiful clothes, and do nothing but amuse herself at the theater and at balls, she would never bemoan leaving a farm. Pigsties and potatoes weren't in it with London! She decided to hold her tongue, however, for if her ladyship wished to talk about farms, she would be most happy to oblige. She had no desire to lose her newly acquired promotion!

Dinner was a festive affair. Lady Winship, much refreshed from her brief nap, gaily fell in with all Lady Carleton's plans for the morrow. Lord Carleton had an engagement at his club, so the three ladies dined alone on a neck of veal, some lobster patties and new peas, as well as numerous creams and jellies. Mariel was delighted with the Carleton's French chef and did justice to all the dishes presented to her. Never had she tasted such food!

Lady Carleton and Lady Winship decided that the first order of business was to visit all the leading modistes first thing in the morning, in order to bring a little town polish to the Winships' ensembles. Mariel was happy to agree, for although she cared little about clothes, she was anxious to see more of London than had been possible during the drive in from Woolwich.

Lady Carleton also suggested that Mariel would benefit from a visit from her hairdresser.

"Not that there is anything exactly *wrong* with your hair, m'dear!" Feeling that Mariel might be offended, she hastened to add, "A more fashionable cut—perhaps some curls?—or smooth?—Henri will know—easier to control! And if cream of cucumber doesn't work, oil of strawberry! Such a pity!"

Mariel was confused. Cream of cucumber? For her hair? She had no time to puzzle it out, for Lady Carleton added, "Also Mariel, beware those jellies and comfits! So dangerous!"

Completely mystified by cucumbers, haircuts, and comfits, Mariel looked to her mother for an explanation.

Lady Winship, her eyes dancing, explained. "I believe dear Daphne is concerned about your weight, my dear! She does not know that you can eat as much as you want and never gain a pound; indeed, she can, Daphne!"

Lady Carleton professed to be relieved as she helped herself to another of the dangerous comfits. The sight of her fat hostess indulging in just the sort of treat she had warned Mariel about was too much for the girl, and she hastily turned away and avoided her mother's eyes.

Lady Carleton questioned Mariel most particularly about her accomplishments. Could she dance? Was she musical? She rode of course, but how well? How many assemblies and balls had she attended? Mariel finally laughed and said, "Dear Lady Carleton, I fear I will be a great disappointment to you! I have not attended any occasion grander than the Harvest Ball at Lord Malcolm's estate near Lochcrae, and hardly any of the family were in residence!"

Lady Carleton was struck dumb by the enormity of the task before her, but Lady Winship said reassuringly, "She is not as gauche as she would have you believe, Daphne! Of course she can dance, oh, not the waltz of course; that has not been accepted in Scotland as yet, but she performs the cotillion and country dances most gracefully. She also plays the piano very prettily and has a lovely singing voice. As for riding, I am sure there is no lady in London who could best Mariel on horseback."

Lady Carleton began to look more cheerful. "We will see about habits immediately then! What say you to a dark bottle green velvet, Ellen? Or should it be pale green to match her eyes? As for the waltz, nothing could be easier; dear Algy can teach her in a morning!" She turned to Mariel and added, "Although you must on no account waltz at Almacks until you have been presented to a partner by one of the patronesses. I intend to get you a voucher as soon as you have met more young people. So hard—no friends—sitting out—no, not to be thought of! Oh dear, I do hope Countess Esterhazy is not so disgusted with me for appearing half-shod on Bond Street that it has not given her a disgust of me! But never mind, Lady Jersey is most amiable! They call her 'Silence' you know, for she never stops talking!"

Both the Winship ladies burst into laughter at this ingenuous statement, delivered as it had been with a tone of reproof for Lady Jersey's failing. Lady Carleton soon saw the joke, and being as good-natured as Lady Winship had remembered, did not hesitate to join in at her own expense. It was a contented trio who made their way to bed that evening, not long after the tea tray had been brought to the drawing room.

Algernon Carleton spent the evening at the Wheatons' reception in a sort of daze. None of the ladies present were as beautiful as Lady Winship; none of the gentlemen's conversation interesting enough to tear his thoughts away from her. The hours before they would meet again seemed to stretch endlessly before him.

When he met John Greeton at the park gates for their ride the following afternoon, he was still in a state of abstraction, for he had spent an unproductive hour trying to compose a poem to Lady Winship's loveliness, and was having a great deal of trouble trying to find an appropriate rhyme for "tender blush." It did not take John any time at all to discover the cause of his friend's frown and vacant blue eyes. Algy was only too willing to tell him all about the angel who had descended into his life. John was treated to a soliloquy on the lady's hair, her green eyes, her graceful form, and her melodious voice, until he was forced to intercede.

"So she was not the fat, dowdy, provincial young miss you expected! It is really a miracle; so often the girls that one's mother expects a son to attend are quite impossible!"

"No, no!" Algy exclaimed. "Not the daughter! Her mother!"

John looked amazed. "The mother? Is she... is she not a trifle—a mere trifle to be sure—too old for you? If she has a daughter of seventeen, I mean?"

Algy frowned. "She is ageless! Such beauty defies time!"

What John thought of this rejoinder he kept to himself, although he wondered if Algy had considered how ridiculous his passion would appear to the rest of the world. Attempting to turn the subject, he asked, "But what of the daughter? What is she like?"

Algy replied impatiently, "Oh, Mariel is nothing out of the common way. She has a tip-tilted nose, a mass of red hair, country clothes, and freckles! And she is pert as well; took me up sharply when I offered the merest commonplace! How the divine Ellen could ever have produced such a poor copy I do not know." He paused and then said, "I wonder if I could use 'gush' or perhaps 'lush'?"

His friend laughed. "I must admit I am all eagerness to meet the paragon that could inspire you to take pen in hand! Even her daughter sounds intriguing. So she took you up sharply, did she? I wager she took exception to the lavender coat! I did warn you, my boy!"

"No such thing; in fact she appeared stunned by my magnificence!" He paused again and then said, "How does this strike you, John? 'Her cheeks divine with tender blush; and when she speaks, all sounds will hush'...?"

"I can only hope all sounds of your poetry would

hush! Good heavens, man, leave it to Byron. He does it infinitely better!"

Algy nobly ignored such outspoken criticism and continued to mutter throughout the remainder of the ride; "'rush'?... no, 'crush'?"

He was not the most amusing of companions in his present state, and John was glad when they reached the gates again and prepared to part, promising Algy he would look in at the theater that evening and see for himself the source of Algy's inspiration. He had another reason for doing so, but this he did not bother to relate to his friend.

Algy gratified his mother by appearing well before time that evening at the Carleton town house. He had thought of bringing a bouquet for Lady Winship but realized that to honor her alone would be insulting to her daughter, and then there was his mother as well. He had no desire to be burdened by three floral offerings which could only make him look ridiculously like a florist shop window. Besides, his poem was not quite finished to his satisfaction, and he wished to enclose it in his flowers as soon as he overcame that one troublesome line.

He was dressed even more magnificently this evening, and Mariel thought he looked much better in the navy he had chosen than he had in lavender! She would have been surprised to learn that Algy also considered her attire an improvement.

The ladies had gone shopping at what Lady Carleton declared a disgracefully early hour, although the Winships, used to the hours at Lochcrae, considered as the middle of the morning. They had been fortunate enough to find gowns for both the Lady Winships to wear that evening, and the modistes had been most obliging about rushing to completion several habits, walking outfits, and ballgowns as well. By the time they had purchased gloves and slippers, stockings and stoles and ribbons, the carriage was full of bandboxes and parcels, and they returned to St. James Square happily discussing their good fortune.

Mariel's gown of soft yellow silk was very becoming, cut as it was with a low neckline, tiny puff sleeves, and a deep gold velvet sash. She had a stole of sarsenet to put about her shoulders and gold silk slippers to match her sash. She had been self-conscious when she donned the gown, for it showed a great deal more of her than she was used to, but Lady Carleton said she would soon become accustomed, and Annie declared it was all the crack!

The hairdresser had spent an hour cutting and arranging her thick red hair, and it was now transformed into a smooth cap that ended in clusters of curls. She was amazed what a difference it made to her appearance. Even the despised freckles had been covered with a dusting of powder.

But if Algy thought her much improved, he did not waste any time considering how it had been done, for Lady Winship, in a sea-green taffeta that matched her eyes, stunned him afresh with her beauty.

He handed her reverently into the carriage after his mother. Was it possible that he had felt her hand gently press his? Oh bliss, he thought as he helped Mariel to her seat. The short drive to the theater passed quickly, for Mariel kept asking question after question of him.

Why were there so many ragged children still about? Surely it was very late for such young ones to be abroad! Oh, what was that building they had just passed? It shone with so many lights; was there a ball being held there? Was it always so noisy in town? Did everyone cry their wares even at night?

On and on she went, and Algy was kept so busy

answering he had no time to do more than smile at Lady Winship.

Mariel was impressed with the size of the Haymarket Theater as they were shown to their box. It was quite as noisy inside as it had been in the streets, and as she took her seat and looked eagerly around, she hoped she would be able to hear the actors.

Algy managed to gain a seat between Mariel and Lady Winship, but was unable to take advantage of such delicious proximity before most of the candles were extinguished, the curtain rose, and the noisy pit subsided a bit as the play began.

After the first act, Mariel turned to her mother, her eyes shining. "Oh, was it not fine, Mama? Dear Lady Carleton, thank you so much! I long to know what will happen to the lady in the next act!"

Lady Carleton patted her hand, delighted her young guest was so pleased. She soon began pointing out people she knew in the other boxes, explaining to Mariel just who they were. Algy wasted no more time, and smiling intimately at Lady Winship, asked her if she had enjoyed her first day in London. It was a brief chat; before long there came a knock on the door and several gentlemen appeared, among them John Greeton, whose nod to Algy seemed to show his approval of Lady Winship's beauty. John paid his respects to Lady Carleton, was presented to Lady Winship and her daughter, and stayed for a few moments to chat. As he returned to his seat in the house, he realized Algy must indeed be smitten, for he had been much too severe about the young lady's looks. John thought her extremely attractive with her gleaming red hair and yellow gown. She reminded him of a marigold, and although marigolds are not exotic flowers, their sauciness and color seemed a perfect comparison. He had liked Mariel's easy manner when they were introduced, for she smiled so pleasantly and talked to him so easily that he had been sorry that he had to leave. He found her refreshing, and although Lady Winship was as beautiful as Algy had claimed, it was clear to him that the lady thought his friend a mere boy, and treated him in much the same manner she would have treated her son.

Mariel, for her part, greatly approved Algy's friend, and she had the irrelevent thought that her Uncle James would have liked him as well.

When the play was over and they had been treated to a farce that Mariel particularly enjoyed, they made their way to their carriage and home. Algy would have liked to take them to supper at Grillons, but when he proposed the scheme, Lady Winship declared she was still rather tried, even as she thanked him for being so kind. He assured her he would be delighted to show her the famous supper room some other time, when she felt more the thing, and went off on wings because in taking leave of him, Lady Winship had not only smiled at him, but had patted his arm as well!!

FOUR

As young Mr. Carleton strolled blissfully along to his rooms, all thoughts of trying to find a convivial card game at the club gone from his mind, he heard himself greeted by one of his older friends and cronies, George Barton. Barton was an older man with a bad reputation as a rake; so bad, in fact, that only his impeccable lineage still assured him entré to the best of society. He was often seen in the company of younger men, for he found them easier to fleece than his contemporaries who had been on the town long enough to recognize his tricks, and as his small inheritance was not nearly enough for him to maintain a luxurious style of living, he added to it by lucky bets and successful evenings at the card table. He was a handsome man, always quietly and elegantly dressed with his black hair neatly arranged; a marked contrast to his weary sardonic eyes and lined face, marked as it was by the pallor of too many late nights and bottles of wine.

He turned aside to walk with his young friend, wondering what on earth had so abstracted him that he had had to call his name three times before he got his attention. Looking sideways into Algy's bemused face, he said jovially,

"I say, dear boy, come along and join me for a drink! What good fortune to meet you when I was just wondering whether to go to the club or look in at Sterling's. Can't for the life of me understand why I said I would attend the party; sure to be a bore! Now we have met I shall conveniently forget it!" He paused and Algy shook his head.

"Not tonight, George! Must beg to be excused! On my way home!"

"Home? At this hour? Are you ill?" his incredulous friend asked. And then, as they passed under a lamp, he added, "I say! Are you hurt?"

Algy looked bewildered. "Hurt? No, of course not, why do you ask?"

Barton chuckled. "Well, you appear to be holding your left arm so tenderly! Come, my boy, you can tell *me!* Have you been fencing and did you drop your guard so your opponent was able to pink you? Perhaps there is a lady in this mystery...".

Algy dropped his hand and blushed bright red. It was true he had been holding his arm at just the place that Lady Winship had touched him, and he was determined that under no condition would he allow his man Pursey to brush that sleeve ever again! He realized that Barton was staring at him keenly, and he replied a trifle wildly, "'Tis no such thing! I don't feel like drinking...or cards tonight! Must ask to be excused!"

Barton saw that whatever Algy had on his mind, he

had no intention of revealing it, and gracefully dropped the subject, talking casually of other things until they reached the top of Whitcomb Street where he bid young Carleton goodnight. He foresaw no difficulty in finding out the cause of Algy's abstraction, and with this in mind, made his way to the previously scorned party.

From another young sprig of fashion he learned that Algy had been seen at the theater that very evening with his mother and two beautiful but unknown ladies. Viscount Sterling confided later that they were relatives of Lady Carleton's, new come from Scotland, and Barton smiled cynically. Perhaps his mother had decided it was time for Algy to be taking a bride and had summoned the girl to be inspected. It certainly appeared that she had found favor with his friend, if his preoccupation and early hours were to be believed, and Barton had every intention of putting a spoke in the wheel if it were possible, for Algy was much too profitable a young man to lose to matrimony and staid evenings spent at Almacks and the quieter balls. He had no doubt he could easily separate his friend from this newly acquired passion and made a note to meet the young lady as soon as it could be arranged.

He did not have long to wait. Some three days later as he was walking in the park, he saw Carleton and a young lady riding towards him and hastened to hail them. As they drew near, he looked the girl over keenly. She was dressed in a dark green velvet habit, very becoming with her green eyes and startling red hair, and she appeared to have no trouble controlling the spirited mare she was riding. Her eyes widened a little when she saw his intense gaze, and she was glad when he turned to Algy, who was accompanying her at her mother's and Lady Carleton's insistence.

Barton was amazed to see Algy looking so sulky. Could it be that he had been wrong in his assumptions, or perhaps the path of true love was not running smoothly, even so soon? He little suspected that Algy had looked forward to an afternoon with the divine Ellen when he magnanimously offered to escort Mariel and was much disappointed when the lady declined, saying she rather thought she would spend the afternoon with Lady Carleton doing some errands now that she knew Mariel would be so well looked after. Even the smile that accompanied this statement had no power to raise his spirits, for instead of riding by his love's side, he was forced to chaperone this pert miss and answer her innumerable questions. He introduced his friend, and Barton swept off his beaver and bowed with accomplished polish.

"Servant, Lady Mary Ellen! Most obedient servant!" he said easily with an intimate smile lighting up his dark face.

Mariel blushed a little. She had never been looked at in such a familiar way, and the admiration in that dark handsome face which should have been so flattering was somehow unpleasant. She replied shortly, and made to ride on, but he put up a hand and grasped her bridle.

"Just a precaution, m'lady!" he said suavely. "Being so new in town perhaps you are not aware how quickly a horse can be spooked, especially such an animal as this!" He turned slightly away from her angry face and addressed his friend.

"I did not see you at Jackson's this morning, dear boy, and I was sure we had made arrangements to meet there. But perhaps it is my lamentable memory?"

Now it was Algy's turn to blush as he recalled the appointment too late. He had sat over the breakfast table well into the morning for he was still composing his poem, and having decided to change "tender blush" to "radiant eyes" had found himself with a whole new set of rhyming problems. He apologized to Barton and a new appointment was made, and then the two friends exchanged a few more pleasantries and Barton related the latest *on dit*. Mariel was furious. After subjecting her to that piercing leer and grabbing her bridle so she could not escape, Algy's friend had ignored her, and she had no desire to sit mumchance while her cousin exchanged gossip with this unpleasant man. As soon as he loosened his grip on her bridle, she dug her heels hard into the mare's sides. This high bred animal was not used to such abruptness, and immediately took exception to it and bolted. Leaving Algy to race after her as best he could, Mariel flew down the row, drawing many astonished cries and pointing fingers as she did so. She did not care; it felt wonderful to ride as she had at home, and it did much to soothe her anger. The pace that Algy had set when they first entered the park had been nothing more than a gentle amble, not at all what she liked. If you wanted to greet your friends and chat, you should walk or ride in a carriage; if you chose to ride, then ride! By the time the mare had quieted down and Mariel was able to hold her to a trot, she had almost circled the park. She halted the now obedient mare and waited for her cousin to catch her up. To her surprise, the gentleman who reached her side first was not Algy, but a complete stranger. He tried to grab her bridle, but Mariel had had enough of that and sharply turned the mare's head aside.

"If you please!" she said quickly. "There is no need for that!"

Her would-be rescuer frowned a little before he touched his hat and said, "Your pardon I am sure! Since galloping in the park is never done, I thought the horse had bolted and you were in danger!"

Mariel stiffened, and replied without thinking, "It would take a better horse than this one to bolt with me!" Feeling this must seem unbearably conceited she added, "Not that she did not try, however! I became weary of riding at a nursery pace, that is all, but I . . . I thank you for your concern!"

At that moment a slightly disheveled Algy rode up, anger at Mariel quickly fading when he saw her companion.

"Your Grace! How kind of you to be concerned for my cousin!" When he saw the noble rescuer had no idea who he was, he added, "I'm Algernon Carleton, you know." He tried to bow elegantly over his horse's withers and was aware that his hair was disarranged, his hat crooked, and his face flushed, and sincerely wished he might have Mariel's neck between his hands for making him look such a fool!

Mariel in the meantime was carefully inspecting the first duke she had ever seen. He sat his horse easily, his strong hands controlling every movement of that impatient animal. He was older than she had thought at first and seemed to be regarding her cousin and herself as wayward children. His face was pleasant without being excessively handsome, and he had a pair of gray eyes and dark brown hair. Everything about him was quietly elegant, and he had a definite air of authority and poise. Mariel decided she liked him, without knowing precisely why. Maybe it was the twinkle lurking in the back of those eyes as Algy introduced her hastily.

"May I present Lady Mary Ellen Winship, Your Grace? Mariel, the Duke of Chatham!"

The duke bowed to her. "Shall we ride on? We are attracting attention here."

The three moved off at a sedate pace, Mariel between the two men, as the duke continued calmly, "I gather your cousin is new to town, Carleton. You should keep her in better order, you know!"

Mariel gasped. How dare he? Before she could reply, the duke said to her, "Whatever is done in the country, setting Hyde Park in an uproar is not generally admired, Lady Mary Ellen. I would advise you to do nothing that so calls attention to yourself, for although you are a superior rider, such antics can only cause the kind of notice that a young woman like yourself is sure to find repugnant."

Algy was red with embarrassment. "Your Grace is of course correct. It is her first ride and I am sure she did not realize..."

As white with anger as Algy was red, Mariel interrupted. "I thank you for your kind concern, sir, but I have little regard for the gossiping of town bloods and Corinthians who appear to me to live extremely worthless lives of no purpose! However, I will try not to *upset* them again!"

The duke smiled kindly at her. "It was just a hint, Lady Mary Ellen, a fatherly bit of advice, if you like. If you wish to be accepted here in town, you are wise to agree to do nothing to set up society's...hmm... worthless backs!"

Mariel would have replied, but he bowed politely, and turning his horse aside was soon riding away from them at a gentle trot.

Algy was mortified. He had never so much as hoped that the Duke of Chatham would ever speak to him, and to have him do so in such a way, as if he were at fault for his cousin's actions, quite prostrated him. He turned to her angrily and hissed, "Now see what you have done! Not content to make everyone in the park aware of your lack of manners, you have had the insolence to spar with the Duke of Chatham! It will be a wonder if anyone receives you or your mother after this, for let me tell you, miss, what the duke decrees is generally accepted. He sets fashion!"

Mariel raised her eyebrows. "How can that be, cousin?" she asked sweetly, "I am sure he was most soberly dressed, not at all as magnificently as you with your primrose breeches and velvet coat! And his cravat was paltry compared to your veritable waterfall!"

Algy opened his mouth to give her a blistering setdown, and as abruptly closed it. The remark he had been about to make would have put paid to whatever chance he had to remain close to Ellen, and in order to be in her company he would swallow a great deal from her termagant daughter. So instead of telling the young lady exactly what he thought of her in no uncertain terms, he bit his tongue and tried to return a soft answer. It was not long before both agreed to terminate their ride, and not many more minutes before Algy was bowing frigidly to Mariel as she dismounted in St. James Square and entered the Carleton house.

Of course the escapade came to the ears of her mother and Lady Carleton at a small dance that evening, and both ladies took pains to tell her the next morning, in their own separate ways, exactly what they thought. She was used to her mother's strictures and took them calmly, but when Lady Carleton fluttered around, waving her handkerchief and exclaiming, "Not at all the thing!—freckles bad enough!—how can I present a hoyden to society?—Oh dear, poor Algy!" and began to cry in distress, Mariel felt badly and promised on her word she would never do such a thing again.

This reassured Lady Carleton until she mentioned it to her niece later. Lady Winship looked up from her needlework and sighed. "Yes, Daphne, I know. She never means to be bad, and she won't gallop in the park again, but I wish we might depend on it that she won't find some other scrape to get into! Perhaps..." she lowered her eyes and smoothed her tapestry carefully as she thought, "perhaps I should have waited another year or two before I brought her up to London for a season, but I could not bear it!"

Lady Carleton did not appear to be confused by this heartfelt statement, and smiled kindly at her niece. "And no wonder, my dear! Buried on that farm...no parties...no company...how you have stood it I have no idea! Besides, Ellen, you must think of the future! Why should you not marry again if you wish to?"

Lady Winship was startled. "I? Marry? Oh no, Daphne, I only wanted Mariel to enjoy herself, and make a good match if she should find someone she loves, but as for myself, I have never considered it!"

She appeared so horrified that Lady Carleton did not persist in the conversation, but she had every intention of looking quite as hard for an eligible husband for her dear Ellen as she did for Mariel, whom she privately considered much too young for marriage. A year or so on the town, and she would be more the thing. And perhaps by then even the freckles might have faded!

The following days produced no new contretemps, and after warning Algy to be most particular about Mariel whenever she was in his charge, Lady Carleton relaxed. James MacDonald could have told her her error.

Lord and Lady Jersey had sent invitations for a ball, and this gave Lady Carleton a chance for even more frenzied shopping. Mariel was weary of the whole evening before she even arrived at the door. Such a fuss over gowns and jewelry and hairdos, she thought scornfully, as Annie and the hairdresser coaxed her brilliant red hair into careful waves and curls and threaded a gold ribbon through them artfully. Her gown was of white, worn over an underskirt of palest gold and banded with matching gold ribbons. She wore pearls and long white gloves and when Lady Carleton and her mother appeared at her door was bade to turn slowly so they might admire the effect. Mariel's face lit up when she saw her mother.

"Oh, Mama, you look beautiful!" she exclaimed, and a little blush appeared on Lady Winship's faultless cheeks.

From the top of her shining golden hair to her silk slippers of palest green, Lady Winship was indeed perfect. She had not wanted to wear the gown for she felt it was not perhaps as matronly as was proper for a mother presenting her daughter to society for the first time, but Lady Carleton was adamant.

"Nonsense, Ellen! There is no need for you to drape yourself in purple and wear a turban, you know! And plumes too, I have no doubt! Everyone knows you were married from the schoolroom. Besides, it is quite the loveliest gown we have seen!"

Lady Winship had to agree, and against her better judgment let her maid hook her into the shimmering pale green silk, cut low over her shoulders to a deep neckline edged in matching lace.

Lady Carleton beamed at them both as she escorted them to the stairs, her deep rose satin swishing from side to side as she descended.

Lord Carleton and Algy stood waiting for them in the hall. Mariel had a smile for the older gentleman for this must be a special evening indeed if he put in an appearance, and as for Algy... She stole a glance at him and could hardly refrain from laughing aloud. He stood speechless, gazing up the stairs at Lady Winship, his mouth open and his eyes glazed. Really, Mariel thought to herself, what a perfect ninny, and even Lady Carleton wondered if perhaps dear Algy was not coming down with something, he looked so feverish.

The ladies' wraps were fetched, the carriage waited, and they were soon on their way through the crowded streets. Lord Carleton complimented Mariel on her gown and said he was proud indeed to present her to his friends.

"And my mother too!" Mariel added quickly after she had thanked him. "For you know sir, this is also her first appearance in London society!"

From his corner of the carriage where he was threatened with suffocation by his mother's bulk, Algy could only agree silently. He had been struck dumb by the sight of Lady Winship in her shimmering gown and wished with all his heart that the poem, so tantalizingly near completion, was even now folded in his coat pocket so he might present it to her that evening. He wondered if he dared to ask her to dance, and hoped that such loveliness did not mean to remain seated by his mother all evening.

Mariel was easy in company now, for she had met many people at parties and receptions, as well as out walking and shopping, and Algy had introduced her to several of his particular friends as well, so she found her dance card filling up rapidly after they had entered the ballroom. There was a considerable crowd present, and Mariel was not at all surprised to see Algy's friend Mr. Barton approaching her. Her mother had turned aside to greet a friend, and Mariel was left to deal with the gentleman herself.

"Lady Mary Ellen!" he saluted her, bowing in his elegant fashion. "May I say you are everything that is lovely tonight? My heart will be broken if you do not grant me a dance!"

Mariel wished she might refuse, but when she looked up at him, she saw such a light of fun and devilment in his eyes that she was intrigued. Gone was the intent leer that had bothered her at their first meeting; here was only a handsome gentleman, impeccably dressed, whom somehow she knew was not in the habit of soliciting debutantes' hands. Surely the other girls would envy her such a distinguished partner! She agreed with a smile and turned to John Greeton who had just arrived. She did not miss the frown Mr. Greeton gave Barton as he left her side, saying fervently, "I live only for that moment, m'lady!"

"Watch what you're about, there, Lady Mary Ellen!" John warned earnestly.

Mariel smiled up at him. "Why, do you know Mr. Barton, sir?"

"Too well," he said grimly. "He is a rake, in case Algy hasn't warned you, and not at all the kind of partner you should encourage!"

Mariel was annoyed. Not only did her mother and Lady Carleton tell her what to do, with Algy forever chiming in with unwanted advice, but now, here was his friend as well! It was too bad!

"I assure you sir, I am well able to take care of myself!" Mariel said haughtily.

Yes, thought Greeton, like a newborn kitten you are! He did not voice this opinion however, but changed the subject and asked her for a dance. Mariel was pleased to comply, for she liked John Greeton the best of all Algy's friends. He was not silly or foppish and he did not give himself airs, quite unlike her cousin she thought gloomily, as that gentleman arrived to lead her out for the first dance.

How exquisite he is, she thought; I am quite cast in the shade, gold and silk not withstanding! Tonight Algy had outdone himself. From his shining blond hair, so carelessly (and carefully) combed in the current mode to his satin dancing pumps, he was a man to be admired. His cravat was tied even more elaborately than usual, his coat of pale blue fit him so tightly he did not look as if he could bend, and the handkerchief he clutched in one hand was edged in at least three inches of lace.

Mr. Barton watched the couple from the side of the room where he was standing with Lord Alverstoke and Viscount Sterling. His brooding stare was interrupted by a deep voice asking genially, "Why George, are you admiring our latest debutante? Not at all in your line I would have said, since she cannot be a day over seventeen!"

Barton looked up to find the Duke of Chatham smiling at him.

"You are correct, sir, but surely even such as I can be attracted to such . . . fresh . . . beauty? Perhaps I have grown wearied of the overripe charms I have spent so much time with of late!"

What the duke might have said in reply was not known, for Lord Alverstoke claimed his attention, and he turned away.

When the dance ended and Algy hurried Mariel back to rejoin her mother, the duke happened to glance their way again, and his eyes widened slightly. He watched Mariel take a seat next to one of the most beautiful women he had ever seen and begin talking to her familiarly. The lady smiled, and at one point tapped Mariel's hand with her fan. When they both turned to look across the room to someone that Algy was pointing out, he suddenly saw a slight family resemblance and made his way to their sides.

Algy was confused by the Duke of Chatham's greeting, and Mariel wondered why he bothered to come across and speak to them since she was sure she must have given him a disgust of her that day in the park. Algy introduced Lady Winship, and the duke bowed.

When Mariel's next partner arrived and she excused herself to dance, the duke remained, chatting easily with her mother and Algy, who refused to be dislodged from her side. Lady Winship was pleased with the duke's attention. Such distinguished address, she thought, and surely he must be taken with Mariel to wish to further the connection after her daughter's behavior at their first meeting. She liked his kind eyes and easy smile, and his courtesy to her as well. Algy cleared his throat at a break in the conversation.

"Cousin Ellen! I beg the honor of a dance!"

Ellen turned from the duke and tried not to frown at the ridiculous boy. Here she was making the acquaintance of a duke who might be the perfect husband for Mariel, and he interrupted, intent on separating them! Before she could deny him, the duke said smoothly, "If you grant him a dance, Lady Winship, I also beg the honor of leading you out!"

Torn between wanting to refuse her young cousin and the desire to further relations with the duke, Ellen agreed.

Algy was in transports, but when the music began he was not so pleased to discover it was to be a country dance, and that he and his partner would be separated in the set almost continually. He was even less pleased when he reluctantly gave her hand to the duke and the musicians struck up a waltz. He glowered at Chatham; how dare he put his arm around the divine Ellen's slender waist!

His eyes never left the couple as they twirled around the room, Ellen laughing up at something the duke was saying, and he thought the music would never end. Lady Carleton beamed happily as she watched. Mariel was not so pleased when the dance ended and her mother brought the duke back to her side and practically forced him to ask her to dance!

"For, my dear," her mother said with a smile and a delicate blush in her cheeks, "I have been telling the duke all about you, and he is most interested in Scotland!"

Mariel glanced quickly at the duke, amazed, but there was nothing but polite interest in his face, so she searched her dance card in confusion.

"I am so sorry, Your Grace," she said, "I do not appear to have any dances left!"

The duke calmly took the little satin folder from her hand and studied it. "You are mistaken, Lady Mary Ellen, for I see the supper dance has not been claimed. How delightful!"

Mariel was completely confused by such distinguished attention, but Algy was quick to take advantage of the duke's move.

"Allow me to take you in to supper, Cousin Ellen! We can make up a table!"

Lady Winship agreed, the duke signed his name to Mariel's card, and bowed and left them. She was very pleased with the turn of events, for Daphne had told her all about the duke after Mariel's escapade in the park.

"Such an old name, Ellen, and so much money as well! The mamas have quite given up any attempt to snare him however, for he has been on the town forever, and although there have been flirtations, and once even a wager when Lady Anne Montagu was presented, he did not come up to scratch. *I* think he has been enjoying himself too much to settle down. He was raised in Yorkshire by an elderly aunt and uncle, and then he served with General Wolfe in the American War, and what with one thing and another, he has not spent much time in town until recent years. Of course he must be all of thirty-eight; I imagine he will be thinking of taking a wife soon and setting up his nursery, if only to preserve the name. The Ainsworths have always been proud of the continuous succession, and I cannot believe that Gregory Ainsworth will be any different!"

Mariel was having a much better time than she had imagined she would. Whirled from one partner to the next, laughing and happy, she realized that life in town could be more enjoyable than she had thought. It was pleasant to see the admiration in a man's eyes, to know he thought you attractive and witty, to have your gown and your dancing applauded. John Greeton brought her back to earth by refusing to pay her any fulsome compliments, but Mr. Barton was positively poetic in his attentions. When the Duke of Chatham appeared to lead her into the set that was forming for the supper dance, she was very pleased, and smiled warmly at him.

"I trust you are getting along better now, Lady Mary Ellen?" he asked kindly, a twinkle in his gray eyes.

"I thank you sir," she said demurely as she curtseyed. "I have done tolerably well I think! At least I have not galloped in the park again!"

He laughed briefly and then asked, "And are you enjoying yourself tonight among such worthless fribbles as we all are, bent only on amusing ourselves?"

Mariel flushed. "It is not kind of you, Your Grace, to remind me of my *faux pas*. Yes, this is most entrancing, but I still maintain that it is wrong for so few to enjoy so much, with little children not a mile away, hungry and cold..."

The duke interrupted. "Surely not cold, m'lady! It is quite a balmy night!"

Mariel would have replied hotly, but he continued, "I am teasing you, of course! It is a shame, but that is the way of the world. I would be interested to hear what you would do to improve matters...."

For the remainder of the dance, Mariel told him exactly what she would do. Starting with the lessons to be learned from the glorious city of Edinburgh and the mistake it was for the poor to leave the clean fresh air of the country for the dirt and smells and disease of town, she progressed through sanitary drains, free schools and better hospitals, and a host of other improvements that according to her could be implemented by any man of vision.

When the dance ended and the duke bent his arm to lead her to the supper room, she stopped abruptly.

"Oh, dear!" she said, "I have done nothing but talk and talk and talk! Why didn't you stop me?"

The duke laughed. "I don't believe I would have been able to if I tried! But I found it very interesting, I assure you. I so seldom hear a young miss in her first season so . . . so vehement."

"Opinionated, you mean!" Mariel said gloomily as he led her to where Lord and Lady Carleton and her mother and Algy were waiting for them. The conversation was general, but Mariel remained convinced that she had offended the duke with her forthright speech! Well, she thought, I don't care! She was glad however that he did not refer to their conversation, for she was sure Lady Carleton would faint dead away if she knew what her great-niece considered amusing entertainment for such a leader of fashion!

The lobster patties, the creams and little cakes and all the other delicacies were much enjoyed, as was Lord Jersey's excellent champagne, although when Mariel held up her glass to the footman for it to be refilled, the duke calmly removed it from her hand and ordered some fruit punch instead. Mariel took it in good part, and his obvious concern for her daughter's welfare pleased Lady Winship very much. She sent him a glowing smile and was even more pleased when he asked if he might call on the Winships the following morning and perhaps take them for a drive in the park.

She left the ball in a dream. Dear Mariel—the Duchess of Chatham! It was like a fairy tale!

FIVE

The following days were ideal, at least from Lady Winship's point of view. True to his word, the Duke of Chatham had called on the ladies, and they had spent an enjoyable afternoon being driven through the park in his carriage. Lady Winship knew they were envied by all the other mothers and daughters who had the felicity of observing them that golden afternoon, and she would have been less than human if that envy had not further increased her enjoyment of the ride.

In addition, the duke never failed to come to the Winships' side at any party they all attended, and although Lady Winship could not quite like the casual, teasing way he treated her daughter, she was content. It was only a matter of time, she thought, before he realized what a treasure Mariel was. She was also impressed by the duke's courtesy to herself. He had such beautiful manners, he never seemed to be dismayed if Mariel was engaged to dance with another, but spent the time happily talking to Lady Winship, and never let his eyes stray towards the young lady with the red-gold hair. Lady Winship made sure her daughter was always dressed in the first height of fashion, with her hair becomingly arranged, and her manners such that even the highest stickler could find no fault with them. Besides, there was Mariel's bright smile and easy manner in company to commend her. She never appeared the least shy or reticent; traits that surely the duke would find childish, such experience as he had. How unlike herself at the very same age! She had been both quiet and retiring and would never have dared to laugh so openly and so vivaciously as Mariel did whenever she was amused.

Mariel would have been amazed if she had known what was in her mother's mind for she never gave the duke more than a passing thought. She had been pleasantly surprised after a few conversations to find that he had both brains and a proper concern for the more unfortunate of the world, as well as a firm grasp on the politics and problems of the day, and that he was not at all adverse to sharing his opinions with her. She admired him; he was so unlike her former idea of a Corinthian, and not at all the fop her cousin Algy was, so she always delighted to see him, but not at all dismayed if he did not make an appearance.

She knew many gentlemen now; if she had a preference it was for John Greeton. She had wondered idly how such a sensible young man could be friendly with her cousin; they were so different. She was always comfortable in his presence, even when he took her to task about some minor social solecism she might have committed, listening to him with good nature, except when he continued to warn her about George Barton. At this good advice she tossed her head and refused to hear him. She found Mr. Barton fascinating. Whenever he asked her to dance, she was always a little breathless, wondering what outrageous thing he would say or do, and to be courted by such a handsome rake was an accomplishment of the first water. He admired her and complimented her, and treated her in such a sophisticated way that she felt quite grown-up. The only annoyance in her life was her cousin's continued attendance. Fleetingly she wondered why, since she was sure he cared as little for her as she did for him. Perhaps Lady Carleton had insisted he escort her because of the family ties. Mariel had quite forgotten her suspicions that he had a *tendre* for Lady Winship and did not connect his smiling good nature when that lady joined them with his silent frowns when she declined to be one of their party.

Algy had not given up his attachment to Lady Winship; in fact, every time he saw her he was struck anew with her beauty, and he worked hard to be sure he remained in her good graces. If that meant he had to spend an inordinate amount of time with Mariel, he was more than willing to make the sacrifice. Actually, as Mariel accummulated a small circle of friends, his task grew easier. He wondered what John Greeton admired in Mariel, and more than once was on the point of asking George Barton what his game was, to be pursuing such a chit of a girl, for he had never seen his friend at all taken by young ladies in their first season. Something always stayed his tongue however, for it would have been awkward to ask such a question of even so close a friend about a member of his family.

At long last he had finished his poem to his satisfaction and was delighted to hear that the Alverstokes were planning an evening of music and recitations to which both the Winships and Carletons had been invited. He toyed with the idea of reciting the poem himself, gazing longingly at the lady as he did so, but came to the conclusion that such attention could only distress and embarrass her; besides, public speaking was not in his line, and he had no desire to make a cake of himself! He forced himself to change the title from "Lines to the Fair Ellen" to "Ode to a Fair Lady" to preserve her anonymity and considered which of his friends he might ask to read the poem for him. No one suitable came to mind; they were all too young and wild, or too young and matter-of-fact to give his lines the emotional reading their quality deserved. He was quite at a standstill until he remembered Sir Percival Rothsbottom with whom he had been at school. Young Sir Percival considered himself a poet equal to Byron and was often asked to read his latest work. How easy it would be for him to include Algy's poem in his performance, announcing it to be by an anonymous newcomer to the literary scene!

Much struck by this fortuitous solution to his problem, Algy called around at Sir Percival's rooms in Clarges Street and was lucky enough to find him in and not engrossed in creating. Sir Percival was astonished to see him, for they had never moved in the same circles, but begged him politely to have a seat and tell him in what way he might be of service. Algy wasted no time in announcing the reason for the visit, and Sir Percival's expression of mild interest soon changed to one of pained horror.

"I say, sir! I could not possibly do so!" he exclaimed vehemently as Algy finished his request. "What? Read *your* poem after my *own* verses?" He shuddered feelingly for he had little confidence in Algy's literary style, however much he might admire his tall, lean physique. Sir Percival was a slight young man of less than average height, much given to pastel shades in his clothing and flowing hair styles, and he had long looked with horror on Algy's set, stigmatizing them as great brutes of no sensibility or learning. He refused to be budged from his decision even when Algy confessed to his state of undeclared love and devotion to the mysterious lady.

"Read it yourself!" Sir Percival sniffed unfeelingly.

Algy lounged against the mantelpiece and eyed the poet thoughtfully, and a look that could almost be called threatening came over his generally good-natured face. Suddenly Sir Percival wished he had had his man refuse Algy admittance, and he sank back in his armchair in something very much like fear.

"No, no!" he said querulously. "It is inconceivable! Think of my reputation, if you please!"

Algy refused to be drawn into a discussion of Sir Percival's reputation and exactly what he thought of it, although he was somewhat in awe of the gentleman's brain now that he knew what devilish hard work it was to write poetry. To think that he had written more than one! And planned to write more! He slapped his gloves hard against one hand as he replied, "Be sure, your reputation will not suffer! You can make arrangements to read it later, and how the devil do you know it ain't any good? Haven't read it, have you? Probably as good as your own; heaven knows it took me long enough!"

Before Sir Percival could point out condescendingly that it took more than time to write good poetry, Algy continued. "Besides, it would be a shame if your mother found out about that little blond bit o' muslin you've been squiring around! She might demand your immediate return to Northumberland!"

Sir Percival grasped the arms of his chair and started to rise. "Why . . . why, that's blackmail, Algernon! How could you?" In his mind's eye he saw his mother descending on London in one of her black rages and whisking him away to obscurity, just when his career was beginning to show signs of being seriously recognized. In fact, he hoped that after Lady Alverstoke heard his verses at her party she would beg to become his patroness, and he had written a special tribute to the lady with which he intended to end his program.

"Call it what you will!" Algy said airily. "I am quite determined you shall read the poem. Come on, Percy! Only you can do it justice!"

Sir Percival was much struck by the compliment and, since he had no desire to be buried in the country again at the height of the season, grudgingly agreed to present Algy's work.

"But *not*, you understand, with my own!" he stipulated.

Algy was happy to agree, called him the best of good fellows, and promised to have the poem delivered well before the evening of the party so as to give Sir Percival time to become familiar with the stirring sentiments expressed.

Lady Carleton was delighted when Algernon offered to escort the ladies the evening of the party.

"Really," she confided to her husband, "dear Algy is becoming so attentive it is most gratifying!"

Lord Carleton had his mind on another matter, as it usually was when he spent any time with his wife, for he had long since given up trying to follow her style of conversation, starting a sentence as it did, and then interrupting with a completely different thought in the middle, and finishing somewhere between the two, and so he agreed absently. If he had considered it at all, he would have thought it the result of his lecture to his son on the advisability of changing his ways.

"I am really quite pleased with him, my dear Algernon," she continued. "Such a help taking Mariel around and serving as our escort on evenings such as this, for, my love, I am persuaded it would not be at all to your taste, although the duke will be there—dear, dear Ellen!—I have such hopes!"

Lord Carleton did not try to untangle this statement, but agreed calmly, saying he was gratified to see such a proper family feeling in his son, something he had not looked for at all.

"Oh well, he is very young, you know—soon settle down—perhaps we are seeing the first indication of it now!"

Lady Carleton beamed with pleasure at this happy thought, and her husband kissed her cheek gently as he took his leave, somewhat cynically thinking that whatever will-o'-the-wisp Algy was chasing now, he was quite sure it was not a burning desire to become a model of conventionality!

Algy arrived promptly, and, as he escorted the ladies to the carriage, chatted lightly of the evening to come. Mariel thought he seemed excited, and after he had monopolized the conversation for most of the short journey, his mother leaned forward and put her hand on his knee.

"Whatever is the matter with you, Algy? Ramblin' on at such a great pace ever since you came! So unlike you!"

"Oh, it's nothing at all," Algy said lightly. "But I warn you, there may be a surprise in store for you all this evening!" He looked meaningfully at Lady Winship as he spoke, but the secret message went uninterpreted since she was searching her reticule for a handkerchief at the time, and merely smiled absently at him when he caught her eye.

"A surprise?" his mother asked in delight. "Whatever can you mean?"

Algy refused to be drawn further, saying only that

they must wait and see. He handed the ladies down at the Alverstokes' door and relinquished them to the butler so they might retire and remove their wraps and repair any damage to their toilettes as had occurred in the few minutes since leaving St. James Street.

Mariel was pleased to see that both John Greeton and the duke were present when she entered the drawing room, although she was disappointed to find that Mr. Barton had not been included. She had looked forward to exchanging whispers with him about some of the performances, for so often he had had her in whoops with his caustic observations on the idiosyncrasies of members of the ton. She had often been hard put to keep her countenance for he was deliciously malicious when he chose to be and, in many cases, extremely accurate.

The guests were eventually all assembled and ushered into the music room where rows of gilt chairs had been placed facing a harp and a pianoforte. The duke, who had been chatting with the ladies, seated Lady Carleton and Lady Winship, and placed Mariel on his other side. Mariel was surprised to see Algy standing against the wall, somewhat in front of them. She heard Lady Carleton whisper to her mother, "Why does not Algy sit down? Plenty of chairs to be had!"

Lady Winship beckoned to him, but although his face lit up, he shook his head and remained where he was. He was soon joined by some other young gentlemen, and Mariel was sure they refused to take seats in order to facilitate their escape if the proceedings became too tedious.

The program began with a young lady playing the harp, who fortunately only presented two short numbers. A portly gentleman was next, his deep baritone completely at odds with his short bandy legs and expansive waistcoat. Mariel was forced to raise her handkerchief to her face at one point when he grew so very red from holding a long sustained note that was well beyond his normal range. She peeped at the duke who was calmly attending the singer, and, aware of her gaze, he turned slightly and quelled her giggles by raising one dark eyebrow. Lady Winship, observing the exchange, was pleased. She had been worrying about Mariel ever since Miss Peckham sat down to the harp. When the baritone had sung the encore entreated by the guests and was bowing to the audience, Mariel whispered to the duke, "How can you remain so . . . so unmoved, Your Grace?"

He whispered back, "I merely think of something *very* serious! For example, the state of the poor, or the machinations of Parliament. While Mr. Hadley was singing, for example, I was deciding whether or not to purchase a team I saw at Tattersall's the other day, and nothing is more serious than that!"

Mariel was much struck by this advice and managed to remain completely composed while a flutist entertained them by wondering whether her Uncle James had drained the marshy field at Lochcrae as he had intended to do and planted it to hay or to wheat.

Shortly before intermission, Lady Alverstoke announced that as a special surprise Sir Percival Rothsbottom would favor them with a poem—"Not of his own composition, you understand, but an anonymous ode!"

The guests, who had been making preparations to adjourn to the dining room and a much welcome light repast before the conclusion of the program, settled themselves once again. Sir Percival had decided after reading Algy's poem that he would present it first, well divorced from his own work, and now he strode forward. Mariel's eyes widened. Even Lochcrae could not keep her from smiling at this vision who took center stage, lounging negligently against the piano. She stifled a giggle as Sir Percival gazed heavenward and waited for complete silence. Truly he was a vision; adorned in peach satin and much foaming lace, with his hair brushed wildly in what he considered a very artistic style, he stood before them. In one hand he held a sheet of paper, and in the other... good heavens, Mariel thought, is that a rose? Sir Percival announced the title and began to read.

It was not so much the sentiments expressed, or the bad verse, that completely undid Mariel, as it was the way Sir Percival recited. He knew the poem was extremely bad, and, in order to save it from complete disaster, he decided to recite the lines emotionally, waving his rose for emphasis. Mariel could not remain calm and buried her face in a handkerchief, her shoulders shaking. This might have gone unnoticed if she had not allowed one very audible giggle to escape her. Algy, who had never taken his eyes from Lady Winship, observed Mariel's behavior from his vantage point against the wall, and he was furious.

Lady Winship ignored the poem as she whispered urgently to her daughter, "Mariel... PLEASE!" The duke added quietly and firmly, "Drains! Think of drains!"

There was polite applause when Sir Percival reached the last line, but he was not solicited for an encore, and the guests soon adjourned, talking together about the evening, and most especially of Mariel's behavior. Algy heard only a few comments about his poem, but those went straight to his heart, and it only made him more furious with Mariel. Not content with ridiculing his efforts so the others could not appreciate his poem, she had distracted the fair Ellen from attending to them as well. It was too bad! Lady Carleton, distracted by the events of the evening, looked around for her son's support as a footman presented a tray of drinks, but he was nowhere to be seen.

Mariel was by now feeling a little ashamed of herself, but when her mother remonstrated with her, she started to laugh again. "Oh, Mama! I can't *help* it! What a ridiculous little man! So... so precious! Does he always carry a matching flower? And that poem!"

She dissolved again, and the duke took a hand as several people nearby turned to look at her disapprovingly. "That is enough, Lady Mary Ellen! You are upsetting your mother!"

His voice was so stern that Mariel stopped laughing immediately. When he saw she was in control of herself again, he smiled a little to remove the sting and added to the ladies, "To be sure, Sir Percival is very young and a trifle absurd! And I must admit that some of the lines—'greeny depths' for example—struck me as an unfortunate choice and caused me great effort in keeping my composure as well! But you must learn, m'lady, that common courtesy demands your polite attention!"

Mariel was much struck by this, and promised to be good. She was glad when John Greeton came up and began to chat lightly, without making any mention of Mariel's *faux pas,* for which she was grateful. How nice he was to hold her hand warmly for a moment and smile at her so kindly in spite of her behavior!

The remainder of the evening was uneventful, even when Sir Percival reappeared to read from his own works. He had discarded the rose and sent Mariel a withering glare. Lady Winship was upset by this, and her heart sank when Sir Percival's aunt, Lady Darwin, snubbed them completely as they left the music room. Even though that nice young Greeton and the duke had remained by their sides, she was sure it was only the duke's exquisite manners that prevented him from leaving them.

She was very wrong. From the first moment he had seen her, Gregory Ainsworth had been attracted to Lady Winship, and, as the days passed and he continued to see her, his admiration grew into love. She was more than just beautiful; she was good, and kind, and gentle. The quietness and reserve that she deplored he found both restful and attractive. It was such a pleasure not to be constantly assailed with wit and vivacity! And that soft, musical voice; those tranquil hands and lovely smile! To think that after all the years he had avoided matrimony with no trouble at all, he should find himself falling desperately in love with a lady who to all intents and purposes thought of him only as a desirable future son-in-law, not a husband! The duke was confused, for he had no idea how to turn her thoughts to their happy union, with Mariel only in attendance as bridesmaid. He had on occasion seen Lady Carleton observing him compassionately, and he felt he had an ally there, but Lady Winship obviously had no idea of his intense feelings, and he was at a loss as to how to proceed. He knew he must continue to dance attendance on Mariel, fatiguing as she was with her youth and high spirits and constant scrapes, as a means to see Lady Winship, and was unaware that he was not alone in this respect. He hoped that by treating Mariel with fatherly kindness Lady Winship would come to understand his real feelings, and took every opportunity he could to fortify this position of elderly mentor. So far, he had to admit bleakly, it did not appear to have done much good. Lady Winship seemed to be of the opinion that he was grooming his future duchess for her exalted position!

Algy appeared at the end of the evening to escort the ladies home, his pale face and subdued manner quite at odds with his earlier exuberance. Lady Carleton thought he had enjoyed a bit more of the excellent punch served at intermission than was perhaps wise, Lady Winship was too miserable remembering her daughter's behavior to even notice him, and Mariel was very subdued, apprehensively waiting for the lectures she would have to endure from both her mother and Lady Carleton and the resulting tears and scenes to which she was sure to be treated.

Nothing more was said about Algy's "surprise," to his great relief, although Lady Carleton startled her dresser the following morning when asked by that worthy lady whether she wished to wear the rose or the blue morning dress by replying, "No! It couldn't be... could it? I don't believe it!"

SIX

The Winships were discussed over many a cup of morning chocolate and afternoon tea in the days that followed. Many ladies felt most sincerely for Lady Winship, especially those with daughters of their own to present to society. If it were not Mariel's indiscreet scrapes, it was apt to be Jane's blushes if a man but looked at her, or Elizabeth's fatal tendency to plumpness, or Meg's dissolving in a torrent of tears if any little thing went wrong, or even Agnes's ability to come out in spots the evening of an important ball. The mamas were sympathetic; on the other hand it was pleasant to be discussing someone else's problems, and not their own offspring's faults!

The chatter might have died down more quickly if Sir Percival had not taken it into his head to castigate Mariel at every opportunity, thus unwittingly feeding the fire. He was sure the minx had quite ruined his chances with Lady Alverstoke, for not only had his own beautiful verses received a mere smattering of acclaim, Lady Alverstoke had not so much as mentioned her desire to become his patroness. And so, on Bond Street and in the clubs and libraries, wherever he found a sympathetic ear, Sir Percival continued to villify Lady Mary Ellen.

John Greeton tried his best to stop these remarks by telling Sir Percival he was making a perfect cake of himself, but the gentleman colored up and exclaimed shrilly, *"I?* I assure you, sir, everyone is most solicitous of *my* feelings in the matter!"

So sure was he that society was completely in accord with his point of view, that he made the mistake of insulting Mariel in Whites one evening when Algy was present in the next room.

Mr. Barton had just dealt another hand of piquet, watched by John Greeton who had wandered over to say hello, when Algy heard that familiar voice say tartly to a friend, "Impossible jade! She should be sent back to whatever Celtic stronghold she came from, yes, and her mother as well! To bring such a hoyden into polite society! Let them both be retired to the savages who consider such behavior as normal!"

Algy uttered an oath, threw his cards to the table, and sprang from his chair to stride into the next room where Sir Percival was seated with friends. Algy's expression was awful as he bore down on the hapless Sir Percival, who, having his back turned, was still regaling his friends with his estimate of the Winships' background. He stopped abruptly when a large, firm hand gripped his shoulder and lifted him from his seat.

"So!" Algy exclaimed through tightly gritted teeth. "You find it pleasant to villify my family, do you?"

Sir Percival gasped and would have replied, except

Algy commenced to shake him so hard he was physically unable to do so. It might have turned into a serious situation except that John Greeton appeared behind his friend and proceeded to take command of the situation.

"Here, Algy, don't be a fool! Put him down! Down, I say! Do you want your cousin's name bandied about even more, as it surely will be if you challenge Sir Percival to a duel? Have a care, man!"

Algy was not so angry that he could not see the wisdom of this and released Sir Percival abruptly, causing him to fall against the table grasping his throat and trying to draw a deep breath. From the doorway, Barton stared at the participants with great interest.

John surveyed the poet scornfully. "I am sure Sir Percival will be delighted to apologize as soon as he is able to speak, and an apology is all that is necessary here, Algy!"

Sir Percival nodded his head violently, well aware that Algy and his friends prided themselves on their aim and ability with both pistols and foils, and tended the desired apology as soon as he was able to do so. Algy stood sternly, his arms crossed, with a mighty frown on his face until the poet was finished.

"Very well, I accept your apology, sir!" he said in a voice still thick with anger. "But let me assure you, if I hear one more remark from you about my family, at any time in the future, I shall know how to deal with you!"

John remarked quietly, but with even more determination, that if Algy were unable to do so for whatever reason, he would consider it a privilege to oblige in his place.

Algy turned on his heel and quit the room, leaving Sir Percival to be comforted by his friends, and indignantly wondering why he was the one who had to suffer, since it was Algy's horrible verses that had put him in this predicament in the first place.

A thoughtful George Barton followed his young friends. It must be serious then, he thought, for Algy to spring so fervently to Mariel's defense. He resolved to double his efforts to detach the young lady from Algy's affections, by whatever means he found at his disposal. How surprised he would have been if he had known that Algy was seething only over Sir Percival's slander of Lady Winship! His assessment of Mariel was in complete accord with Algy's own feelings about the young lady. Savage Celtic, that she was, indeed!

Barton poured a glass of wine for them all and begged Algy to take up his hand again, congratulating him on his forbearance and good sense until Algy relaxed and preened himself on his masterful handling of the affair. John also congratulated him, and the evening might have been most enjoyable from that point on if Algy had not felt the need to constantly return to the incident, reminding them both of his patience and tolerance and strong sense of family duty. As it was, the party broke up at a rather early hour.

Lady Carleton had been very thoughtful for several days, often lost in abstraction when her husband or Ellen spoke to her, but as time went by, she recovered her good spirits and was as delighted as Lady Winship to see the duke still faithfully in attendance.

Mariel had completely forgotten the episode, for she had a new scheme in mind. Ever since she had seen the incomparable Miss Hamilton driving through the park in a very dashing phaeton behind a spirited pair, and with only a small tiger up behind, she was determined to do so herself. She was sure Lord Carleton would lend her a team, once he was convinced she was capable of handling his horses, and bent her mind towards finding a suitable instructor. She mentioned her plan to Mr. Greeton one evening as they were sitting out a dance and said she rather thought she would ask Algy to teach her to drive.

John laughed out loud. "No, you won't, m'lady!"

"And whyever not, I should like to know?" Mariel replied, indignant that he thought her unable to drive a team.

"For one thing, my dear friend is not only one of the worst drivers in town, he is completely unaware he is so ham-handed, and drives at a breakneck pace, tempting fate every time he takes the reins!" John told her, brutally castigating his friend's skill without a qualm.

"And furthermore, he thinks himself well up to the nines, with his driving skill top of the trees, and cannot understand why the Four Horse Club will not accept his membership! No, not Algy, not if you value your life, m'lady!"

Mariel frowned. If not Algy, then who could she ask? At that moment the duke appeared, and her face lit up in such a warm smile that John, taking his leave, glowered jealously.

"Whatever is the matter with young Greeton?" the duke asked mildly as they took their places in the set now forming.

"I have no idea!" Mariel said blithely, her mind searching for a way to propose her scheme. Caution, however, told her it was not a propitious moment while the duke was minding his steps and so often separated from her in the dance. She smiled winningly at him when they came together, and was so charming that the duke was alarmed, wondering what on earth she had on her mind now. Her Uncle James would have applauded such caution.

Mariel did not have a chance to speak to the duke that evening, for he did not return to her side, but she was content to wait. It seemed he was always around; perhaps he would call in St. James Square soon and she could ask her favor.

The following morning, her mother asked her to return a book to Hecton's Library, and since Mariel needed a few small things as well, she was delighted to oblige, and ran to the breakfast room to ask Lady Carleton if she had any commissions for her. The lady hugged her for her thoughtfulness but declared she could not think of a thing, which caused Lord Carleton to put down his fork and ask his wife if she was sure she was feeling quite well.

Lady Carleton ignored the sally and reminded Mariel to ask Ridgeway to have the carriage brought around and to be sure to take her maid with her and a footman as well, to carry her packages.

Mariel assured her that she and Annie could manage by themselves and hurried off upstairs to fetch her pelisse. It was a beautiful morning, and both girls were glad to be abroad, even if it were just for the purpose of library books, a new pair of silk stockings, and a bottle of Denmark Lotion.

The streets were crowded that morning, and it was some time later before the coachman drew up before Hecton's Library. Mariel blithely dismissed him.

"It is such a lovely day, I have decided to walk home, Ames! And with all the crush in the streets, I am sure we will reach St. James Square before you anyway!"

The coachman grinned and tipping his hat, drove away. That Lady Mary Ellen! She was a spark, make no mistake about it!

Annie insisted on carrying the new book her mother had ordered, and in complete harmony both maid and mistress purchased the lotion and several pairs of stockings in a delightful bazaar in Oxford Street. Finding themselves near the end of the street, they turned down Picadilly for the walk home, Mariel chatting lightly to her maid, and setting a brisk pace.

As they turned into St. James Street, Annie hesitated and put a hand on Mariel's arm.

"Oh no, m'lady, we cannot go this way! Whatever was I thinking about to let you head this way? You will have to walk by all the gentlemen's clubs, and it isn't done, no, not at all...."

Mariel stared at her in dismay. She was feeling a little tired, and her new slippers of jonquil kid were not as comfortable now as they had been when she so carelessly dismissed the coach. Her lower lip came out as she surveyed the street before her. It was such a short distance to the square, and such a very long way around! Her mind made up, she started forward again, her maid close behind her, still protesting.

"Oh hush, Annie! I am sure 'tis not as bad as you say, and besides, it is still very early. All the fashionable gentlemen will very likely still be in bed!"

That did not seem to be the case however, for several gentlemen ogled her as she walked along, and a few went so far as to turn and raise their quizzing glasses. Mariel's cheeks were burning. There was still quite a way to go to reach the square, and she did not think she could bear to continue, but surely to turn around would be even worse! She would have to run the gauntlet of men who had already subjected her to such close scrutiny. She decided to turn down Jermyn Street, and quickened her pace, the faithful but still protesting Annie at her heels.

As she turned the corner, she ran full tilt into a portly elderly gentleman who, having amply breakfasted, was making his leisurely way to his club. Taken by surprise, the gentleman tried to avoid her and, tripping over his cane, fell down on the street, uttering a loud "woof" as he did so. Mariel clutched at Annie, sending her packages flying, but the two girls managed to steady each other. Mariel impulsively knelt next to the gentleman and offered to assist him to his feet, exclaiming, "Oh, my dear sir, I would not have had this happen for the world! It was *all* quite my fault! Do let me help you, please!"

The gentleman, whose face had grown alarmingly red, eyed her with loathing.

"Get away from me, you young mopsy! Pon rep, things have come to a pretty pass when a man cannot even walk down Jermyn Street at eleven of the clock without being set upon by the likes of you!"

He shook off Mariel's helping hand with disgust and hoisted himself to his feet.

"I beg your pardon, sir," Mariel said coldly, now as white as he was red. "I fear you mistake the matter. I am Lady Mary Ellen Winship, not... not a MOPSY!"

Behind her, Annie moaned. Why, oh why did m'lady have to tell him her *name?*

"Ha!" the gentleman replied, brushing himself off as best he could. Taking his beaver from Annie's trembling hand, he set it firmly back on his now somewhat disordered white locks.

"That's what *you* say, and you can call yourself anything you like, but Lady Anybody, you are not! No *lady* walks down St. James Street!"

He harrumphed in triumph at this indisputable fact, and, before a horrified Mariel could explain further, began to call loudly for the watch.

"I'll have you taken up for assault and... and soliciting, that's what I'll do!"

"Annie, gather up our packages quickly," Mariel hissed, praying with all her might that there was no officer of the law within earshot. The gentleman seemed to have a very carrying voice for such an old man, and she certainly did not want to have to explain

88

to either her mother or the Carletons why she had been consigned to Newgate!

The old gentleman puffed off around the corner in his search for the law, and Mariel prepared to run for her life, just as a familiar voice behind her exclaimed, "Lady Mary Ellen! What on earth are you doing here, and whatever is amiss?"

She whirled to see John Greeton staring at her in astonishment.

"Oh John!" she wailed, feeling immeasurably better to see his handsome face. "You are a lifesaver! Do you hear that elderly man calling? I am so afraid he is going to have me arrested for assault, for as I hurried around the corner, I knocked him to the pavement, and he is extremely angry!"

"Then we should not delay for a moment!" John said, firmly repressing the many questions in his mind. "Here, girl," he said to Annie, as he handed her a package that had rolled into the gutter, "let us be off!"

The trio hurried away down the street, and Mariel did not feel a bit safe until they turned the corner on Duke Street. She stopped for a moment to catch her breath, while John turned to make sure they were not being followed.

"No, we are in luck! The coast is clear!" he reassured Mariel, his hazel eyes now twinkling.

"Thank heavens you came along when you did, Mr. Greeton," Mariel said more formally. "I can never repay you for your help!"

"Oh, yes you can, my girl! You can explain how this all came to pass!"

Ignoring this familiarity, Mariel was only too happy to oblige, and soon the whole story came tumbling out. "But it is my fault, not Annie's," she concluded, "for she said it was not the thing to do, but I insisted!"

"Perhaps it was not quite the thing, but since the

gentleman does not know you, he can hardly bandy your name about!" John said.

Annie moaned again, and Mariel blushed crimson. "Oh, but he can, John! I told him who I was!"

"Now whyever did you feel you had to do that?" John asked, somewhat stunned by this piece of bad news.

"Well," Mariel replied, her head high, "he called me a 'mopsy,' and although I am not perfectly certain what that signifies, I am sure it is not in the least complimentary, so I felt I must set him straight!"

"Thereby making him feel better for being knocked flying by a member of the ton, and not just any old commoner?" Greeton could not resist asking. When he saw her frown at this bit of levity, he added quickly, "It is most unfortunate that you mentioned your name!"

Mariel began to walk again. She was tired and out of breath, and her eyes were prickling with tears, and all she wanted to do was reach home safely so she might have a good cry! Besides, her feet hurt most abominably! Why she had ever thought these stupid slippers were becoming she would never know, she thought crossly, as Annie trailed after her, and John hurried up to offer his arm. Drawing her hand closer, he patted it kindly with his other hand and said, "Well, Mariel, it is done now. Allow me to escort you home, and then perhaps it would be helpful if I return to the clubs and find out if the gentleman remembered what you said. If he was so very upset, perhaps he did not hear you correctly."

Mariel brightened at this thought. The elderly were so often hard of hearing, perhaps she might yet escape from this coil without a word of it coming to her mother's ears. As they reached the Carleton town house, John bowed over her hand, and she felt much better, and thanked him again with a pretty smile.

"There is one thing more, Mariel," John said. "Perhaps it is *outré* of me to ask, but I feel I must know! What is that very pungent scent that has been accompanying us all this way?"

Mariel looked confused, but Annie spoke up. "'Tis the Denmark Lotion, m'lady! The bottle broke when it fell in the gutter!" At this statement she burst into tears, as if that too was somehow her fault, and in soothing her and helping her into the house, Mariel missed the warm, intent look John gave her as he prepared to retrace his steps.

Unfortunately, the old gentleman did not forget her name, and the *on dit* spread like wildfire up and down St. James Street. It would not be unfair to say that George Barton helped fan the flames, for he was one of the first to hear of the incident, and could hardly believe his good fortune. Here, at long last, was the perfect means to separate Algy from the Lady Mary Ellen, for young and careless he might be, even he could not condone the behavior of a girl who had the audacity to stroll boldly down St. James Street and upset an elderly gentleman to the point where he was sure to bandy her name both far and wide. Barton smiled. What a beautiful morning it had turned out to be! He was very busy that morning, and it was not long before everyone in polite society was aware of Lady Mary Ellen's latest start, and once again the gossips had a new scandal to chew over, along with their angel cake and macaroons and afternoon tea.

Mariel was quickly made aware that she had not escaped unknown, for when Lady Carleton returned home that very afternoon from a card party at Lady Peckham's, she went immediately to bed, not before, however, summoning Lady Winship to her side.

Lady Winship soothed and calmed her and put her to bed in a darkened room with her vinaigrette, her salts, a cordial, and several large handkerchiefs, after which she called for Lady Carleton's maid to sit with her mistress. Behind the serene manner she adopted for Daphne's benefit, Ellen was extremely angry and upset. How could Mariel *do* this, she wondered. It was almost as if she set out to make their stay during the Season impossible! She did not for a minute believe that Mariel was doing it deliberately, but she remembered how loathe her daughter had been to come to London, and wondered drearily once again whether she had been too precipitate in bringing her out so soon. Lady Carleton's dresser, Wiggans, appeared and Lady Winship prepared to seek out her wayward daughter immediately. The dresser said, "Begging your pardon, m'lady, but Ridgeway asked me to inform you that the Duke of Chatham has called and begs a word with you."

Ellen put her hands to her head in a distracted way, disarranging a few soft curls. "Oh no!" she exclaimed. "I cannot see him now! But perhaps...? Yes, I will!"

Without going to her room to check her toilette, she hurried down the stairs and entered the small salon where the duke was waiting for her. As she hurried in, he thought he had never seen her looking so beautiful, even with her hair disarranged and wearing a very plain morning gown. Her green eyes sparkled, and anger had brought a rosy blush to her face that caused her gentle beauty to bloom.

He bowed over her hand and she burst into speech without thinking.

"Your Grace! Have you heard? Is it indeed true?"

The duke did not appear to be confused by the question, and nodded his head soberly. "Yes, I fear Mariel has done it again!" he said. "But come, sit down! Have you not spoken to her yet?"

Lady Winship obeyed him, sinking down on a small sofa and beginning to wring her hands. "No, I have just this minute come from Daphne—Lady Carleton, I mean—for she has had to be put to bed she is so distraught! But Your Grace, it is good of you to call! I am quite prepared for all our acquaintance to cut us dead, from this point on!"

She moaned softly, and the duke leaned towards her. "My dear Lady Winship, allow me to order a glass of Madeira, and then perhaps we should have the young lady join us? I would like to hear the story of this morning's escapade from her own lips! And I assure you, your friends will not cut you dead. At least *one* friend will not!" He smiled warmly at her as he spoke, and went to summon the butler to bring the wine and ask the Lady Mary Ellen to join them.

Lady Winship relaxed and sipped her wine. She did feel better, and a good deal more calm, and if the duke were not going to cut the connection, perhaps all was not lost. He *must* be in love with Mariel, she thought, to condone this type of behavior! I hope she realizes what a wonderful man he is! Suddenly she felt very depressed, for no reason she could name.

It was a very subdued Mariel who joined her mother and the duke a few minutes later. Lady Winship shed a few tears during the proceedings, and the duke, although standing impassively by the fireplace, wished he might have the schooling of Lady Mary Ellen for just a few moments so that he might punish her appropriately for so upsetting his love! He was pondering whether whipping her or boxing her ears would give him the most satisfaction, when Lady Winship appealed to him.

"Your Grace, whatever can we do? Please give me your advice, for I am at a loss as to whether to remove from town immediately or concoct some illness to explain our disappearance from society!"

The duke was startled. The thought of the Winships

leaving town had never occurred to him, and the fact that they would probably return to Scotland and never be seen again was too terrible to contemplate. Why, Lady Winship would be lost to him forever!

He smiled at them both and said, "Come, come, m'lady! 'Tis not that bad! I would suggest you remain and brazen it out. In a few days everyone will have something new to gossip about, and although a few of the highest sticklers might cut you, I am sure my credit is good enough to carry you through if the ton sees we are still good friends. Do you attend the Brixton ball tonight?"

Lady Winship nodded her head, and then said, "Perhaps I should send our excuses; I know Daphne will not be well enough to come, and..."

"By no means should you fail! I shall be there by your side, you know!" Recklessly he sent her another warm, caressing smile, but Lady Winship was staring doubtfully at her daughter.

"I am not perfectly sure that that is the wisest course," she began slowly, but Mariel interrupted her.

"Oh, Mama, I am most dreadfully sorry, but I quite see the duke is right! It would be... *cowardly* to turn tail and run!" She rose and went up to the duke, holding out her hand and smiling shyly.

"It is too good of you, Your Grace, to support us. I was so afraid that my behavior, although I did not *mean* to be bad, would cause you to desert us, and I would have no further opportunity to ask you for a most particular favor—that is, I mean..." She stopped in confusion as the duke raised one dark eyebrow.

"A particular favor?" he asked slowly. "I know the correct thing for me to say, and say quickly, is 'your favor shall be granted, m'lady! Anything in my power to do, etc. etc.,' but knowing you even such a short time has made me cautious! You must forgive me if I ask first, *what* favor?"

Lady Winship rose from the sofa and came towards them quickly, her breath coming fast, and a look of anger on her face.

"How *dare* you, Mariel? I am ashamed of you to be asking anything from the duke after all he is prepared to do for you! I forbid you to speak!"

The duke laughed. "I think, Lady Winship, we had better hear what this young minx has in mind, in order to prepare ourselves for—hmm—for whatever consequences might ensue. Knowing the young lady, I am sure there will be consequences! Come, what is this 'favor'?"

Mariel eagerly told him of her desire to learn to drive a pair, and begged him very prettily to teach her, "for," she said, "I know that you are most skillful with the reins, Your Grace, and under your tutelage I could learn very quickly!" She looked up at him and saw his frown, and so she added, "I did think of asking Algy, of course..."

The duke interrupted. "Absolutely not! That is all we need, you and Algernon overturning a phaeton in the park!"

Mariel demurely agreed that she had heard that perhaps Algy did not have the expertise of the duke, and that gentleman said dryly, "No need to empty the butter boat over me, Lady Mary Ellen!" He turned to Lady Winship and added, "I think it might be a very good idea, m'lady. At least we will know where she is, and I shall take the greatest care of her, you know! And when she is on the box, she cannot be strolling down St. James Street upending elderly gentlemen, or galloping through the park!"

Lady Winship said faintly that he was too good, and

he took his leave, adjuring them once again not to fail to appear at the Brixton ball.

When he was gone, Lady Winship rang a mighty peal over Mariel's head, and sent her to apologize most humbly to Lady Carleton. She herself remained in the salon thinking about the Duke of Chatham, and his unending kindness! To think that he would take on the added burden of teaching Mariel to drive! Surely now her daughter would see how wonderful marriage to such a kind, considerate, handsome, and masterful gentleman as the duke would be! She wondered once again, however, why such happy thoughts should cause her to feel so depressed, and shaking her head in confusion, resolved to put them out of her mind while she went upstairs to choose the gowns they would both wear to the ball that evening.

SEVEN

The Brixton ball was an evening of acute discomfort for Lady Winship, the duke's almost constant attendance notwithstanding. She could hear the whispers, see the turned shoulders, hear the sniffs, and she was extremely sorry she had ever allowed the duke to convince her that they should come. She kept her feelings hidden however; at eighteen she would have wilted and retired in tears; now she appeared calm and self-possessed, holding her head regally high. No matter what the gossips said, Lady Ellen Winship would ignore it!

She had dressed very carefully for the evening in a new gown of pale lime-green, and Lady Carleton had begged her to borrow an emerald and diamond set. Feeling that such a magnificent blaze of jewels would lend her courage, she had accepted the offer gratefully, but when she finally came to say good-night to Daphne, she wished again that she might remain at home and bear that lady company.

Lady Carleton would have none of it. "Pooh, Ellen! You look splendid, the emeralds are perfect with that gown! Besides, you did promise the duke after all. But for heaven's sake, keep an eye on that daughter of yours!"

She moaned and sank back on her pillows, and Lady Winship kissed her gently and departed. Mariel was very quiet; there was no need for anyone to watch her that evening. Her mother had chosen a demure gown of white for her to wear, and if you had been seeing her for the first time, you would have thought her a pretty, behaved young lady, although a trifle shy. The duke eyed her cynically as they danced together.

"Come, Lady Mary Ellen! There is no need to present this nunlike saintliness, you know!" he said tartly. "Especially when everyone here knows it for the lie it is! Smile, if you please! Do you want more gossip? The guests will be thinking I have said something most improper from your shrinking demeanor!"

Mariel looked up at him and tried to smile. "I do not mind what they say about me, Your Grace, but I am very concerned for my mother. She *does* care about society, and I fear that the ton may castigate her simply because she *is* my mother. That is what is so hard to bear!"

The duke silently agreed that such a situation would be intolerable, but he only replied, "Well, you are very young after all, and there is no one in this room who has not committed his or her share of youthful follies! I could only wish that it had been anyone else but Toddles Bellington that you knocked down this morning, for he..."

Mariel interrupted him. "Did I hear you correctly, sir? TODDLES?"

She had to laugh when the duke explained that Mr. Bellington had received his nickname some years ago from the singular way he had of walking, and went on to say that he was a very warm man, quick to take offense, and constantly deploring the informal manners of the younger generation. Such moral laxity had not been so in his time, as he so often pointed out to his long-suffering friends and acquaintances. He had talked to anyone who would listen about his experience of the morning, and there was scarely a person in the ton who had not heard about it by nightfall. Mariel looked around the room cautiously, but Mr. Bellington was nowhere in sight, for which she was extremely grateful.

Algy had of course heard the story, and his handsome mouth had tightened in annoyance. How dare Mariel do something so *outré!* He had presented himself at St. James Square especially to accompany the ladies to the ball, and stood close beside Lady Winship, scowling at anyone who looked her way. He knew how to protect her! Since Mariel was not asked to dance by anywhere near the number of gentlemen who had formerly solicited her hand, she was often seated beside her mother as well, and to George Barton it appeared that not even the Lady Mary Ellen's latest mishap had the power to shake Algy from his devotion! He wondered what measures he should use now to separate him from the young lady. After the morning's contretemps he had looked forward to a quiet game of cards for very large stakes with Algy this evening, and there he was, not at all disgusted, but practically glued to the Winships' sides! He strolled over and asked Lady Mary Ellen to dance, wondering if he should play rival lover for Algy's benefit, something he was sure he would find extremely tedious. He quite agreed with Toddles that the young were an abomination!

He also wondered idly why the Duke of Chatham

saw fit to champion the Winships, but he did not believe, as the rest of London society did, that it was Mariel's attractions that inspired him to such devotion. Rather he decided the duke was captivated by Lady Winship, for even he had to admit he had seldon seen a more beautiful woman!

He teased Mariel a little until her spirits revived, treating the whole thing as a famous joke, and telling her all the outrageous things Toddles Bellington had claimed had happened to him, and Mariel was very scornful of such exaggeration.

"One would think I had injured him permanently!" she said sharply. "And when I think he had the effrontery to call me a 'mopsy,' well! I am sure I have just as much reason to be offended as he does!"

Barton encouraged her to continue in this vein, and it was not long before Mariel was feeling sure in her mind that she had been injured quite as much as Mr. Bellington, if perhaps not more so!

When John Greeton came to dance with her, she was much like her old carefree self, a circumstance that caused John to look at her askance. When he questioned her, she told him what Barton had said, and he quickly restored her to a proper frame of mind by saying in a crushing way, "Yes, yes, that is all very well, but remember that it was your fault after all. *You* were where you did not belong, *you* knocked the old gentleman down, and do not, for heaven's sake, continue to use the word 'mopsy'! It is most improper!"

Mariel's eyes widened. "You mean a mopsy is—is...?" She stopped in confusion as John's handsome face reddened.

"That is just what I mean, and you will have the goodness to stop talking about it!" he got out, and then deliberately changed the subject. Mariel was horrified by Mr. Bellington's assessment of her station in life, and highly indignant as well. How *dare* he? But for John to give her such a set-down dampened her spirits again, and it was a very subdued young lady who finally took her place in the Carleton carriage for the ride home.

Algy, declining to so much as talk to her, pointedly chatted only with Lady Winship, who had the headache and wished most sincerely that her young cousin were not so endlessly attentive! She thanked him for his support however when he escorted them to the door, and smiled kindly at him, and Algy went home determined to show the lady that his love and devotion were forever at her service.

The days that followed were a welcome island of calm for both Lady Winship and her aunt. Mariel was unbelievably good. She rarely ventured from the house, and then only in the company of her mother. Lady Winship returned her own books to the Circulating Library, and Lady Carleton sent her own dresser to purchase a new bottle of Denmark Lotion for Mariel. The only entertainment that she attended without her elders was a picnic at Richmond. She was accompanied there by both Algy and John Greeton, neither of whom left her side; Algy because he did not trust her out of his sight, and John because that was where he most wished to be.

In time society began to forget, a circumstance helped along by a Mr. Wilforde's challenge to a member of the peerage, the duel inspired by that same peer's attraction to Mrs. Wilforde, and even Toddles Bellington did not refer to the matter again more than once or twice a day.

Lady Carleton was encouraged, but still she sat down and wrote to both Lady Winship's sisters who had not come to town for the season, proposing a visit from Lady Winship and her daughter possibly in the near future.

"It is not that I do not wish my dear Ellen to remain with me for as long as she wishes," she assured her husband, "and who can say what irremediable damage might be done if she had to leave town just now, but it would be provident to have family to visit just in case Mariel should do something else truly outrageous... oh dear, I shudder to think what it might be!"

Lord Carleton applauded his wife's foresight, but was inclined to think she took the matter too much to heart. She declined to argue her case. She knew Mariel a great deal better than a man who saw her so seldom and was always inclined to excuse her because he liked her youthful playfulness and high spirits.

Lady Carleton also bemoaned the necessity of keeping their distance from the patronesses of Almacks. "It is too bad, Ellen," she confided, "but I would so much rather not ask for vouchers at this time. How mortifying if Countess Esterhazy or even Lady Jersey should refuse us! Much better not to ask at all, don't you agree?"

Lady Winship nodded absently. She had another problem on her mind, and, although she was sorry that Mariel should be denied access to that most guarded of portals, she was much more concerned with the identity of the gentleman who was continually showering her with gifts of flowers and expensive trifles.

The flowers had started arriving the morning after the Brixton ball, and, as there was no card, she could hardly return them. Since then, every morning, there was another offering, sometimes accompanied by a heartfelt line extolling her beauty, but never signed. She had wracked her brain trying to discover which gentleman she had inadvertently encouraged and could think of no one, for she had kept herself very much in the background to increase Mariel's chances of a good match. A gay widow could not be considered a proper mother-in-law after all!

Lady Carleton thought it a very good joke, as did Mariel, and there was much merriment about "Mama's secret admirer" from that young lady until Lady Winship forbid her to tease again.

Unfortunately, the Duke of Chatham paid a morning call one day just as Ridgeway was staggering away from the door under the weight of a large urn filled with a multitude of blooms at least three feet tall. When Lady Winship came downstairs to greet the duke, the butler presented her with the accompanying card, and she looked at it quickly, her color rising as she read the fulsome compliment it contained. There was no way for the duke to ask her who had sent such a monstrous thing, and, as she did not offer any explanation but merely led him into the salon until Mariel could be informed of his arrival, he was left in the dark. He found his temper rising and a feeling of such jealousy in his heart that he was hard put to chat lightly of this and that with pretended nonchalance.

When Mariel entered the room, Lady Winship excused herself for a moment, something she had been doing with great regularity every time the duke called, to his great annoyance. Today however, he was glad when she left the room and, after setting a time the next afternoon for Mariel's driving lessons to begin, asked casually about Lady Winship's admirer.

"Is it not amusing, Your Grace?" Mariel gurgled. "Poor Mama! She has not the least idea who is sending the flowers and gifts for they are never signed! And something comes every day! Sometimes there is a card pledging undying devotion, and sometimes a bit of verse. Whoever he is, he does much better when he goes to the classics for his poetry, for his own attempts are woefully funny! Mama will not let me tease her anymore, but since there is no way for her to send the gifts back, she is forced to give them house room." Mariel laughed again, but the duke's strong hands clenched tightly into fists at the information.

"Well, and why not?" he asked mildly when he had control of his voice. "Your mother is a beautiful woman after all! It is not to be wondered at that she should have admirers!"

This was a new thought for Mariel who considered everyone over the age of thirty to be getting on in years, but she hastened to agree with the duke. After all, he was going to teach her to drive, and she wished to remain in his good graces.

The duke toyed with the idea of sending flowers to Lady Winship himself, but was forced by the circumstances of their relationship to forego the notion. It was a shame, for he would liked to have showered her with attention. To be forced to stand in the background, unable to attempt anything of the sort, was surely the first time in his long career that he had been so frustrated. He seethed about it inwardly. If he could have done so, he thought he would like to send her creamy yellow roses, a flower he identified with her. He would have quite agreed with John Greeton that Mariel was like a marigold, pert and brilliantly colored, but her mother was most like a long-stemmed rose in full bloom, a magnificent flower with its satiny petals and soft, delicate scent.

If the duke was chafing under his enforced silence regarding his feelings for the lady, so too was Algy. Sending the flowers and gifts had been at first a balm to his heart, but it was becoming increasingly difficult not to throw caution to the wind and let the lady know who her admirer was! Of course Lady Winship never mentioned the mysterious offerings to him, but he had the gratification of seeing them many times in the various salons and in the drawing room of the Carleton house. He did not connect their appearance there with the fact that Lady Winship would not have a one of them in her own bedroom and boudoir, no matter how handsome they were, and all the fans and handkerchiefs and bottles of scent were given to the maids as soon as she opened the package. Annie was delighted, and even Lady Carleton's dresser watched for the daily delivery with a great deal of interest.

Society buzzed when it was seen that the Duke of Chatham was taking up the Lady Mary Ellen for a drive just about every afternoon thereafter. This was such distinguished attention that some of the more venturesome plungers were betting that Ainsworth had at last succumbed, and who would have thought it would be a pert miss, barely eighteen if she were a day, who was constantly in trouble? Algy was too much wrapped up in his own concerns to pay much attention, but John Greeton frowned heavily when he heard the talk. One evening, therefore, he sought her out, determined to find out her true feelings for the duke, and was startled as he drew near to hear her chastising Lord Lawrence for his continued stay in town when she knew, she said, that he had extensive estates requiring his guidance.

Lord Lawrence, a middle-aged man of exquisite taste who was always impeccably attired in the latest fashion, was seldom found anywhere near those estates, for he much preferred the gaiety of town, and he was beginning to look much affronted.

Lady Mary Ellen pointed out to him tartly that a landowner had a duty to his property and his tenants, and she quite wondered that he and so many others could bear to waste their time amusing themselves during the season with balls and parties when it was obvious they would be much better employed riding around their holdings and checking the crops and livestock. John Greeton hastily intervened and led her away, leaving a much discomforted and angry peer behind. When Lord Alverstoke and the Duke of Chatham came up and greeted him, he said indignantly, "As if I had the least interest in hay or potatoes or pigs! Besides, the country is so... so dirty!" He shook out his ruffles and bristled while the duke and Alverstoke exchanged bewildered glances.

"And then there's manure!" he added, in a voice of extreme loathing.

"There is always manure!" the duke got out. "What on earth are you talking about, Clarence?"

Lord Lawrence explained, and Alverstoke shook his head over the lady's folly in lecturing Clarence Lawrence, a man who set fashion and had a large crowd of followers among the ton. The duke also sympathized, but at the same time felt no small amount of admiration for Mariel that she would defend her beliefs so fervently. He tried to point out how praiseworthy this was, but Lord Lawrence interrupted him with a sniff.

"Naturally, *you* are bound to defend her!" he said.

The duke frowned a little and would have disabused his friend of the notion there was anything between him and the young lady, but Lawrence was called away before he could marshall his thoughts. It was unfortunate that Lawrence then felt called upon to relate the story throughout the evening, and heads were mournfully shook over the impossibility of ever civilizing the Lady Mary Ellen.

John led Mariel to a sofa somewhat apart from the main crush. As she sat down, she smiled at him warmly, but for once he did not return it. Instead, he asked abruptly, "And what was that all about, and to what purpose? Don't you know that Lord Lawrence rarely leaves town, and has no interest in his estates, except for the very good income they produce for him?"

Mariel tossed her head. "More to his shame, then! I should think myself amiss if I did not point out his failings, yes, and every other gentleman who had tenants depending on him! He should be ashamed of himself!"

John sighed and shook his head. "As it happens, I quite agree with you, but why do you feel *you* have to be his mentor? He is several years older than you, and it is most rude of you to take him to task! Sometimes, Mariel, I wonder if you will ever reform!"

Mariel looked down at her hands folded in her lap. "I fear I am impossible, John! It is just that I miss Lochcrae so much, and this endless season goes on and on, and there is no sign of mama's bringing an end to our visit. Are we never to go home?"

She looked so woebegone that he wanted to take her in his arms and comfort her. Instead, he asked her to tell him about Lochcrae, which of course she was delighted to do. They remained together for some time, until Algy came to fetch her to her mother, and when she had gone off on Algy's arm, John knew a great deal about her Uncle James, the prize flock he was raising, and all Mariel's favorite places on the farm. If other young ladies had their heads turned by all the amusements and gaiety of London, Lady Mary Ellen Winship was not among their number. John smiled fondly to himself until he remembered that he had quite forgotten to ask her about her daily drives with the duke.

The lessons were coming along very well, as even the duke was quick to admit. Mariel had a deft hand with the ribbons and never jobbed at the horses' mouths, but she never allowed them any freedom in deciding exactly how they should go, for she was in complete control. Her years at Lochcrae had developed a strong pair of hands as well as a good understanding of animals. The duke had not yet allowed her to drive his prize chestnuts, but he promised her the day was not far distant, if she continued to improve at the pace she had begun.

Because of the lessons the duke was thrown a great deal more into her company and was surprised when he began to feel a genuine fondness for her. She was so honest, so happy and gay, and she had such an intriguing way of looking at London and its ton that he often went home in a great good humor after their lesson. Mariel was not above pointing out various members of society and giving a very astute view of them, for she seemed to feel she could confide in the duke freely. The driving lessons kept her busy, and since she was behaving very well indeed, everyone at Carleton House relaxed, everyone that is but Algy who continued to keep a very close eye on her, cynically refusing to believe her sudden good behavior was at all permanent.

It was just as well he did, for he heard her one evening agreeing gaily with George Barton that the season was becoming excessively flat, and an evening spent at Ranelegh at a masked ball open to the public was just exactly what she had always wanted to do, and she would be delighted to accept Mr. Barton's escort. Algy himself had been to many such entertainments, and he knew very well how improper they were for a young lady in her first season, even a most circumspect and retiring young lady. What Mariel would do there did not bear thinking about, being neither circumspect nor retiring! It was all right for a young blood to go and ogle the bits o' muslin that were sure to be there parading their charms, but it was the outside of enough for a lady of the nobility to so forget herself. She would be subject to all sorts of unwelcome attentions from men of the lower classes, and Algy, for the first time looking at his friend in a new light, did not feel Barton's chaperonage would be at all adequate to keep Mariel in check. Why he had ever proposed it was a mystery, but Algy determined to put a stop to it immediately, and as soon as George had strolled away to fetch Mariel a glass of negus, he was at her side.

The conversation that ensued was conducted in harsh whispers, with a great deal of head tossing and "I will!"s on Mariel's side, and many head shakings and "No, you won't"s on Algy Carleton's. After he had rung a mighty peal over her head, sarcastically reminding her of all her past misdeeds once again, Mariel was forced to agree with him that perhaps it was not the thing to do after all, especially since Algy did not mince any words describing exactly what happened at masked balls open to all.

When George Barton had forced his way through the crush of people with her drink, he found the lady alone, and was surprised to discover she had changed her mind about the proposed expedition, and no amount of teasing or enumerating the treats in store could get her to reconsider the invitation.

He was a little disappointed, but since he had begun to consider the Lady Mary Ellen's downfall a personal challenge to his ingenuity, he retired to plot other methods, now that this particular ploy had failed.

EIGHT

More and more, Lady Winship began to hear people talking about leaving town, now that the season was fast approaching its close. Whenever she heard a conversation about the relative merits of Bath or Brighton or one of the other watering spots, she frowned a little, for the duke showed no sign of asking for Mariel's hand; if anything, he was more casual with her than ever, and although she had heard him call her daughter "Mariel" once or twice, she realized that that was not enough to build up any hopes. It was maddening; what was wrong with the man? After all, he had been monopolizing all the girl's time these last few weeks, and if there had been any other suitors—and here Lady Winship had to admit honestly there were none that she knew of, with the possible exception of John Greeton—perhaps the sight of his endless attentions had scared them away. It would be a very conceited young man who thought himself the equal of the Duke of Chatham, and young Greeton was not in the least conceited! Not that she meant to encourage that match, not with the duke in the picture! Then too, she was feeling a little uncomfortable with the length of time she and Mariel had been in St. James Square. She resolved to ask Daphne what the Carletons' future plans were, and to make arrangements to return to Scotland, visiting her sisters in the country on the way north. Whenever she determined to do this, her spirits sank. She had had such dreams for Mariel! Perhaps if she waited just a bit longer!

One morning as she was returning from some shopping, she was distressed to see the shutters being put up and the door knocker removed on the house next door. She stared at this definite sign of yet another departure and then looked around. Yes, the Crandells across the Square had left too! She sighed as she went into the house, seeking her aunt out as soon as she had removed her bonnet and sent her parcels upstairs. Lady Carleton was seated in the small salon she often used in the morning, poring over a large batch of bills.

"My dear Ellen! Did you find the lace you were searching for?" she asked, sweeping the bills inadvertently to the floor as she turned to greet her. Lady Winship knelt and gathered them up as her aunt continued, "Thank you, my dear, so clumsy of me, but then, I hate bills! Always have, always will! And these lie! I am sure I never spent half the amount this quarter! Such a good thing Algernon is wealthy, for I have not the least idea of economy, and the price of things is outrageous!"

Lady Winship put the bills back on her aunt's desk, and Lady Carleton tried to arrange them neatly in a halfhearted way.

"Eighty pounds for candles! One would think we burned them night and day! And tea and hay and liveries and coal and wine and wages and silver polish! I must ask Ridgeway if he has the least idea how much silver polish he requires; I am sure it is excessive! But there." Sweeping her neat pile of bills untidily into a drawer and slamming it, she said, "Let us not think of them again!"

Lady Winship had to laugh. "Do you think, dear Daphne, that they will disappear because you have hidden them away?"

Her aunt snorted. "Not in the least; they will be more likely to multiply, there in the dark! Remind me to give them to Algernon as soon as possible before they have a chance to do so!"

Lady Winship sank down in a chair next to her aunt and, taking a deep breath, asked her about her plans for the rest of the summer. As Lady Carleton looked at her inquiringly, she added, "You see, dear aunt, I know I should be making arrangements to leave town too, and I intend to do so—" She sighed, and brushed an errant curl back. "But oh, I had such hopes! However, if Mariel did not take, there is nothing more to be done. But the duke—well—I am sure it is no wonder I have been hoping that he—that Mariel—oh dear, it is too depressing!"

Lady Carleton did not appear to be at all confused by this disjointed speech, perhaps because she so often spoke that way herself.

"I know you did, Ellen, but so have I, and I can assure you they are vastly different from yours!" Lady Carleton patted her niece's hands and chuckled a little. "Oh yes, very different indeed, and *my* hopes are not at all cut up! As for leaving, it has been quite impossible for us to make any plans since Algernon is kept in town yet awhile on business. Perhaps later we may all repair to Brighton; yes, that might be a good scheme, if nothing happens before that which I am quite in hopes it will—so close to his estate, it would be a very good thing! I shall call the agent and have him start looking for a suitable house on the Front for us...."

Lady Winship interrupted. "Oh no, Daphne, you cannot mean to continue to house us! Why, you have been most kind to allow us to remain as long as you have! And I do think it would be a very hard thing to get Mariel to agree to Brighton when she is pining to return to Lochcrae! If *only* the duke..." her voice trailed off, and Lady Carleton said briskly, "Yes, if *only* the duke! Just what *I* had in mind! Do not despair, we have a few weeks yet, and he shows no sign of leaving town, does he?"

Lady Winship said that he had not confided any such plans to her, or to Mariel that she knew of, and began to look more cheerful at the thought that there was some little time left. Lady Carleton wondered out loud if perhaps she might not give a small dinner party some evening soon, as London began to thin of company, and of course include the duke in the festivities, and Lady Winship left her making out a list of guests on the back of one of the despised bills.

As she regained the hall, Ridgeway bowed to her and presented her with a small parcel, neatly tied with ribbon.

"This has just come, m'lady," he said repressively.

"Oh dear, not another one! Ridgeway, did you ask the boy who brought it if he could return it?"

"I did inquire of the young person as you requested, m'lady, but he gave me a cheeky answer and made off before I could insist!" Ridgeway sniffed, and looked even more disapproving, if that were possible, remembering the sass of the dirty urchin that he had been forced to deal with. It was not at all what he was used to!

Lady Winship sighed again and took the package. There was a bulky letter attached, and with some hope of finally discovering the gentleman's identity, she opened it there in the hall. It was addressed to the fair Ellen, and asked her to be kind to one who had for so long worshiped her from afar. The writer pledged eternal devotion, love, and etc. etc. which went on for several flowery paragraphs. Then he asked her to meet him early that evening in a secluded part of St. James Park so that he could finally acquaint her with his name, and have the privilege of falling to his knees before her and ... Lady Winship crumpled the letter in disgust. Why did she have to attract this kind of trashy devotion, and *who* could it be? Suddenly she resolved to settle this once and for all, and went up to her desk where she wrote a scathing reply to the mysterious gentleman, telling him that his attentions were most unwelcome, and since she had no intention of *ever* meeting him, she begged to inform him that any gifts that he continued to send would henceforth be thrown away unopened as soon as they were delivered; any bouquets would be dispatched to one of the London hospitals as well. She signed it with a flourish and asked her maid to give it to one of the old grooms, who might be able to identify the man, along with instructions as to where and at what time he should reach the appointed tryst. Feeling a great deal better for her decisiveness, she gave the unopened package to the maid for her trouble, and told her to tell the groom that if he were successful, he would be handsomely rewarded as well.

Hetty, the maid, crept up to her room to open the gift, and was delighted to discover a beautiful gold locket, inset with a single diamond.

"Whew!" she said to herself, for she had been expecting another bottle of scent, and she already had four such bottles from Lady Winship's admirer. "Coo-ee! This is something like!"

Opening the catch, she saw a lock of butter-blond hair tied to a velvet ribbon which she discarded immediately. Since her favorite of the moment had black hair, her callousness was perhaps understandable. She carefully hid the locket under her mattress before she went down to the stables to speak to the head groom, Albert Dortle.

Dortle had been born on the Carletons' estate and grew up there, for his father had been head groom before him, and he was perfectly content to continue the line, coming up to town with the family every season, and overseeing the stables when they returned to Oak Grove, their country estate. Since all the servants had been following the affair with a great deal of interest, he assured Hetty he would be glad to help the lovely Lady Winship, and shook his gray head at the folly of her impetuous suitor.

Early that evening, he made his way to the designated place and retired behind a bush to wait. Fortunately it was not raining, and, even though the light was fading fast, he was sure he would be able to identify whoever came to keep the appointment, or at least, he told himself stoutly, get a good description of the man, such as would permit the lady to discover his name.

Several minutes passed, but Dortle was not perturbed for he had come quite a half hour before the appointed time, to be sure to be out of sight. At last he heard hurried footsteps approaching down the winding path and peered eagerly through the branches of his bush as a man came quickly around the last bend, looked searchingly around, and then sighed with the satisfaction of finding himself first. Dortle's mouth fell open.

"'Ere, now, is that you, sir?" he croaked.

Algy whirled. There was no one in sight, but someone had clearly spoken from behind that bush! He approached it cautiously.

"Who is there?" he asked, trying to sound stern and in command.

"I don't believe it!" the bush replied.

Algy flushed and stepped forward. "Come out of there at once and show yourself! Who are you?"

The bush rustled, and Algy stepped back quickly. It was, after all, a deserted part of the park, and it was getting darker every minute. He wished he had his cane or his sword stick with him, but one did not rush to meet one's love clutching a weapon! Dortle came from behind the bush and stared at Algy, and it would have been quite a contest as to which was the more astonished.

"DORTLE?" Algy croaked in disbelief.

"SIR?" replied Dortle.

Dortle recovered first. He had been expecting a man after all, while Algy could in no way reconcile Dortle's gristled features with Lady Ellen's delicate face.

"'Ere now, sir, was it you wots been sending the lady all them folderals?" he asked, sternly folding his arms across his chest.

"Yes, it was, Albert!" Algy admitted. "But why are *you* here?" He wiped his brow nervously.

"I'm 'ere at Lady Winship's request! She give me a letter for you, m'lord, and I wuz to discover who you might be if I could, as well. WELL! Never would I 'ave believed it, never in all my born days!" Dortle shook his head in disbelief, and Algy saw that his case was desperate, and hastened to reply.

"See here, Albert, you must not tell her who I am, do you understand? It would ruin everything! I see there has been a misunderstanding here, but I would not let the lady know this way that I love her!"

"Love 'er?" Albert asked, his eyes wide in astonishment. "'Ow can you love 'er? She's almost old enough to be your mother, sir!"

"Never mind that!" Algy snapped. "Just you take yourself off home and pretend you didn't know who I was! Tell her the man was short and fat with red hair and a full beard if you have to, but for heavens' sakes, do not let her know my name!"

Dortle began to chuckle. "Aye, and 'ow many short fat redheads does the lady know, I wonder? Use your 'ead, sir! I'll make up a story, but 'ere, 'ere's 'er letter to you, and best you read it carefully, and stop apestering 'er! The Lady Winship wants none o' you, my boy!"

Algy ignored this sudden familiarity, for Dortle had known him since he was first breeched and had put him up on his first pony not long thereafter. Besides, he was going to be forever in his debt after this escapade! He thought of promising him a goodly sum but refrained, just in time. Albert Dortle thought himself as much a part of the Carleton family as Algy did, and such a promise of largesse could only cause offense.

He was still chortling as he hurried away, leaving a disconsolate Algy behind, clutching the lady's letter and lamenting his misfortune. Algy had been chafing for some time because his gifts and notes were in no way advancing his cause. One night, he even woke from a deep sleep and sat up in bed abruptly, thinking that perhaps dear Ellen might feel it were some other gentleman and favor his suit. Since that time he had been more particular in his writing, hoping to give her the hint. If Lady Winship had not stopped reading these epistles, she might easily have guessed, Algy having a very heavy hand with a hint, but she had long since consigned all cards and notes to the fire unopened.

Algy felt heartsick as he made his way back to his

rooms. All for naught, all for naught, he told himself drearily, and it had been so very expensive! All those flowers and gifts, and that locket he had sent today! He shuddered when he remembered the cost! But at least, he consoled himself as he handed his hat and gloves to Pursey, she would not know from Albert Dortle that his young master was the man! All was not lost, at least not yet.

He sat down to read Lady Winship's letter, fortified with a glass of wine, and was relieved to discover that at least it would be of no use to send any more expensive gifts. He dined alone, in deep thought, and went early to bed, quite forgetting an appointment he had made with George Barton to play cards at Whites that evening. He had no idea how he was going to advance his suit now, but perhaps the morning would bring fresh counsel.

Dortle reported to Lady Winship in the small salon as soon as he returned to St. James Square. He removed his cap and smiled kindly at her as she rose anxiously and began to question him, but he had to admit he had delivered her letter to a stranger.

"No one *I've* ever seen before, m'lady!" he assured her, piously forgetting every precept he had been taught about honesty being the best policy.

"But what did the man look like, Dortle? Surely you can remember that!!"

"Oh, aye," he agreed, scratching his head. "He was about my 'eight I'd guess, and dark complexioned—dressed fine as ninepence he were, m'lady, and lands! He was some upset you 'ad not come! Oh, and one more thing, he was an older man—that is to say, in his fifties, I'd wager!"

Feeling he had covered Algy's tracks as best he could, he smiled again while Lady Winship took a turn about the room, deep in thought. She could not immediately call to mind anyone who fit the description.

"Did he have no unusual characteristics, Dortle?" she asked finally.

"Characteristics, m'lady?" he echoed in confusion.

"Yes, you know, like a beard or a wart or a long nose...?"

Sorely tempted to invent a bushy moustache and a peg leg, Dortle managed to stifle his imagination. "Not that I could see, m'lady, but it was growing dark and 'e wore a beaver pulled down over 'is eyes, so mayhaps that was why I don't recollect 'im better!"

Lady Winship sighed and seemed so disappointed that Dortle added, "At least 'e won't be abothering you anymore, m'lady! I told 'im it were no use, and 'e 'ad your letter when 'e left!"

"I hope you may be right, Dortle!" Lady Winship said, but when she would have paid him for his trouble, he refused.

"No, no, m'lady! 'Twouldn't be right, for after all, I wasn't much 'elp to you, now was I?"

No amount of insisting could change his mind, and Lady Winship went up to dress for dinner in a very disappointed frame of mind. It was so frustrating not to know who the man was, and so very intriguing to have a secret admirer, no matter how clumsy his tactics! Perhaps Dortle was right and the unwelcome gifts and flowers would cease to arrive every morning, for the gentleman was sure to be discouraged by her stern letter. She was able to console herself that she had done all that she could for the present and resolved to put the whole thing from her mind.

She had to be spoken to more than once at dinner, however, for she was very absentminded, her thoughts tending to turn over the mystery when she should have been listening to Mariel or Lady Carleton. Mariel could not help teasing her a little, and soon had the whole story.

"But how exciting, Mama! How could you *bear* not to keep the appointment? Why, I would have been there right on the minute, just to see who it might be!"

Lady Carleton nodded her head and said, "Yes, I am sure you would have, my girl, and found yourself embroiled in another adventure before the cat had time to lick her ear! We can only be thankful that you were not the object of this mysterious gentleman's love!"

Mariel laughed at Lady Carleton's horrified expression and leaned over to squeeze her hand.

"Dear Aunt Daphne! I am a sore trial to you both, am I not? But you must admit I have been very, very good lately!"

Lady Winship congratulated her daughter, but Lady Carleton, looking through a dish of comfits, said gloomily, "I wish it did not give me palpitations wondering when and what you will do in the near future, for such meekness and propriety cannot last!" She shook her head, and Mariel hastened to reassure her that she had nothing whatever disreputable on her mind.

Even so, Lady Carleton would have been horrified but not a bit surprised if she had seen Mariel the following evening playing piquet with George Barton in a small room removed from the ballroom where she should have been dancing. Lady Winship and her aunt were deep in conversation with Mrs. Wheaton and her young cousin who had just arrived in London and had the felicity to live near Lady Winship's older sister in Burton-Upon-Trent and was able to relate all kinds of stories of the family and how they were faring. Lady Winship was delighted to hear that dear Mary's oldest daughter was about to be married and that her nephew Reginald was going up to Oxford in the fall, so it was some time later when she realized that she had not seen Mariel for some time. She was about to excuse herself and go in search of her when she saw the duke escorting her back into the ballroom and she was able to relax.

The duke, who had also noted her absence, had disengaged himself gently from a conversation with some other gentlemen and gone to seek her out. He found her gleefully adding up her winnings, watched indulgently by Barton. Since they had been playing for pennies, her share was of small value, but she could not have been more pleased if she had won hundreds of pounds! The duke reminded her of the dance she had promised him, and, with a gay smile for Barton, she allowed him to lead her away. As they joined the dancers, the duke said casually, "You spend a great deal of time in George Barton's company, Mariel! A word of advice; do not be so much with him; he is not at all the kind of man you should cultivate!"

Mariel looked up at him in amazement. "Why, Your Grace, he is a friend of yours, is he not? And he is very big with my cousin Algy!"

The duke corrected her. "He is an acquaintance of mine, surely, but not one of my cronies. George Barton is a man forced to live by his wits and whatever means he can find to separate younger men from their money. I believe he is currently bent on such a course with young Carleton. He will make any wager, and his play at cards is notorious! He has never been caught cheating, for if he had been, even his impeccable lineage would not be enough to save him from expulsion from the ton, but..."

"I think it is too bad!" Mariel interrupted, her color high. "If he does not cheat, perhaps he is only lucky! And for you to accuse him, with no proof, of... of leading young men astray is really too much! Besides, *he* was not lucky tonight, *I* was!"

The duke did not reply for a moment, and then he said easily, "I believe it is the way of men like Barton to allow their victims to win at first. Tell me, did he suggest you might enjoy an evening at a discreet card party given by a dear friend of his?"

He was watching her closely as he spoke, and saw her guilty start.

"Just so! On no account are you to go to such a house! They would fleece you mightily!"

Mariel tossed her head, but she was disconcerted, for Mr. Barton had indeed suggested such an outing, although the appointment was for the following afternoon. Mariel had assured him she could escape surveillance and join him at Mrs. Peggoty's, and, after her success at piquet, was sure her good luck would enable her to make a great deal of money. She had even imagined repaying her mother and sending the rest to her Uncle James; and now, here was the duke saying she must not go! She frowned a little and he added sternly, "If you do not give me your word, Lady Mary Ellen, I shall be forced to refer this matter to your mother!"

Mariel peeped up at him and saw that his normally pleasant face was very stern, and there was no twinkle now in his handsome gray eyes—they were positively wintry! She forced herself to promise, and then she added darkly, "I don't know what business it is of yours, Your Grace! Why, you are lecturing me exactly like a parent!"

The duke laughed and bowed as the dance ended. "Exactly, dear Mariel! I am, after all, old enough to be seen in that light, so you must forgive my high-handedness in the matter. Besides, if I find you have not kept your promise, the driving lessons will cease immediately!"

Mariel was indignant. "You have my word, the word of a Winship, sir! I shall not go to Mrs. Peggoty's tomorrow!"

Following her from the floor, the duke could be heard to mutter, "Mrs. Peggoty's! Good God!"

Mariel ignored him as she joined her mother's party, but later that evening she made a point to speak to Mr. Barton again and begged to be excused from the card party. She had been in quite a quandary as to how she was going to manage this when she had been all eagerness only a short time ago, but now she said that friends from the country had arrived in town and her mother wished her to help entertain them. Barton assured her it was no great matter, but when he tried to arrange another time, she became distressingly vague, saying that the duke had first priority since he was teaching her to drive. Barton was annoyed although not a trace of it showed in his dark, handsome face. Algy had failed to keep their appointment last evening, and Barton was no closer than he had ever been to separating Algy from his bewitching cousin. There was nothing he could do, however, to force her to play cards with him so he changed his tactics and asked her how the lessons were coming along. Mariel proudly told him she was to try the duke's chestnuts soon, and Barton applauded.

"Why, m'lady, if Ainsworth allows you that privilege, you are become a veritable whip! What say you to a curricle race? I do not pretend to be as good a driver as the duke, but I believe I could give you a good race. Perhaps with a handicap, since you are so new to the game. I wager that even with a head start I could contrive to beat you!"

Mariel was intrigued. She was confident she was as good as most men with a team and was sure she could beat Barton, so she agreed to consider a race seriously. Lady Winship came up then and claimed her daughter, for their carriage had been called for, and Barton went away well pleased with his new scheme, and sure she would accept his challenge.

True to his word, the duke allowed her to drive his chestnuts only a few days later, and Mariel was much on her mettle to prove she could handle such a skittish pair. When she had negotiated the crowded streets, and managed the narrow park gates without mishap, she dropped her hands and let the team settle into a fast trot.

"Bravo, m'lady!" the duke said, smiling at her. "That was very well done indeed!"

Mariel returned his smile and was extremely careful with the team until they returned to St. James Square. Then she asked the duke innocently, "Have I passed your stringent test, sir? Would you agree now that I am a capable whipster, able to drive to an inch?"

"Perhaps not to the inch, Mariel, but certainly to the foot!" he replied, laughing at her eagerness. It was at times like these that she was most appealing.

"Well, I accept the foot, for *now*," she agreed. "I am sorry that our lessons are at an end however, for I do not believe that Lord Carleton has anything to match your chestnuts in his stable! He did say I could borrow a team as soon as you agreed that I was able to handle them without coming to grief! *Please* tell him so when you see him!"

The duke agreed to do so, and when the Carleton town house was reached, Mariel transferred the reins to him and nimbly stepped down from the curricle without help, thanking him once again, and, tripping merrily up the steps, went to inform her mother of the duke's approval of her skill.

Those of the fashionable set who remained in town had the pleasure a few days later of seeing Lady Mary Ellen, seated in Lord Carleton's curricle, competently tooling his team of grays through the park, attended only by Albert Dortle, who sat with his arms folded, looking completely unconcerned about his fate.

Lady Carleton had had her doubts of the wisdom of allowing Mariel this freedom, but her husband said she was being gothic, and if it made the young lady happy, he considered it a quite unexceptional pastime. He had heard of her prowess from the duke, and he himself had gone for a drive with her before he agreed.

"She is really very competent, Daphne, and it is not as if it were a perch phaeton and she was driving it alone! Of course she really wanted only a small tiger up behind, but one of the conditions I made was that Dortle must accompany her. Do not fear! I am afraid you are becoming irrational where Mariel is concerned!"

Lady Carleton bit back the retort she had been about to make and subsided.

That evening, Mariel saw George Barton at a party. He congratulated her on her emancipation and on her skill, and reintroduced the idea of a curricle race. Mariel was torn between accepting the gauntlet thrown down to her, and listening to a small voice in her head that warned her repeatedly that she must not on any account do this.

Barton began to discuss the route, as if her acceptance were a matter of course, and she was intrigued in spite of herself. The run he proposed from London to Warlingham could be accomplished easily with no need for a change of teams, and leaving plenty of time to return home before anyone missed her. I am sure I could do it and win, and with no one the wiser, she said to herself.

You know very well you should do no such thing, her conscience said sternly! Barton could see she was wavering, and applied a little more pressure in the form of a gentle taunt.

"Can it be that I have been mistaken in you, m'lady? Perhaps you do not have the courage, or perhaps you have less confidence in your driving skill than I thought?"

That was all that was needed to make Mariel put up her chin and accept the challenge, stifling the flutter of uneasiness she felt at her daring.

Barton said he would be happy to arrange for the rental of two teams, as identical as possible, and insisted she have first choice in order to be fair. He also insisted she have a five minute head start, and she was violently denying the need for this when the pair of them were overheard.

Unfortunately it was Sir Percival Rothsbottom who was passing the alcove where they were talking, and he had never forgiven Mariel for her treatment of him. He sniffed in scorn as he heard her—and with that rake Barton, too!—planning a race to Warlingham. Just what he would have suspected, he thought, from such an ill-bred, uneducated minx! He decided it was none of his business, and resolved to put the whole sordid episode from his mind.

If only it had been the duke, or Algy, or even John Greeton who had wandered by at just that moment, all would have been well, with Mariel only smarting a little from the thundering scold any one of those gentlemen would have been delighted to administer!

Unaware she had been overheard, Mariel agreed to a wager of fifty pounds. Fifty pounds you do not have, the small voice whispered. Oh hush, Mariel said to herself, I intend to win! The small voice subsided in defeat, and the only problem in Mariel's thoughts as she went to sleep that night was the possibility of rain on the appointed day, three days hence.

NINE

If the day of the race was not bright and sunny, at least the clouds massing overhead looked as if they might hold off the rain they threatened until late afternoon. Mariel dressed early that morning, helped by a very uneasy Annie, who had not only been told of the race, but informed she must accompany her mistress. She had tried to demur, but Mariel said on no account could she go alone; she was not as dead to all proper feeling as that!

"For I know," she confided, "that although racing between a lady and a gentleman is not much done, surely no one can find anything amiss if I have my maid with me!"

Annie could have told her it was not done at all, but she saw Mariel would not listen to reason, she was so sure she could win the race and be back in the house before anyone wondered where she had gone. Annie gave up protesting and agreed to the scheme.

"We will win, I know it, Annie!" Mariel said gaily as she sipped a cup of chocolate. "And you are not to worry about the extra weight because you are along, for I imagine the two of us do not even equal the bulk of one tall gentleman!"

Annie, folding away Mariel's pegnoir and nightgown, shook her head, for weight was the last thing she was worried about!

The two girls left the house in plenty of time to reach the rendezvous. Mariel was relieved that neither her mother nor Lady Carleton had come downstairs yet. She left them a brief note explaining she had gone out to purchase some new kid gloves for the ball that evening, and had taken Annie with her, and they were not to look for her until late because she was going on directly to the Misses Wiltwicks for luncheon and an afternoon of silver loo. All quite unexceptional, she thought smugly, for I do not want them to worry! But she had to admit to herself that it was easier to write the lies instead of looking into her mother's clear green eyes and speaking them.

The posting inn Barton had named as the start was reached by hackney coach, and during the drive there Annie tried again to convince Lady Mary Ellen that it was not too late to back out and return home. Mariel was horrified.

"I have accepted a challenge, Annie! I cannot fail— why, every feeling must be offended!" For, even if it were wrong to be engaging in a curricle race with a noted rake, she added to herself, that was in no way as bad as reneging once the wager had been made.

In the meantime, John Greeton was entering his club, hoping to find Algy there. Algy had been very much depressed since his meeting with Dortle in the park, and had even wished—where his spirits were especially low—that he had never had the misfortune to fall in love after all. It was extremely unpleasant, and not at all what he had imagined, as he confided freely to John. He had taken to imbibing a bit more brandy than was good for him while he pondered his problem, and John was worried about him. He was deep in thought, therefore, as he stepped into Whites, and in the darkness of the hall stumbled into a gentleman about to leave. Stepping back to apologize, he recognized Sir Percy, and nodded distantly.

Sir Percival bristled and would have passed him without a word, except John absentmindedly took hold of his arm.

"Have you seen Algy Carleton about, by any chance, sir?" he asked, for if Algy was not there at Whites, he would seek him immediately at Brooks.

Sir Percival drew himself up to his entire five feet six.

"I wonder that you care to continue to associate with any member of the Carleton family, sir!" he said, "especially after what the Lady Mary Ellen is about to do! But I perceive you are as dead to shame as any of the rest of them!"

He tittered angrily, and John peered at him more closely.

"Whatever are you babbling about, Percy?" he asked, taking a firmer grip on the gentleman's sleeve in case he decided to bolt for it. Sir Percival was aware he had gone too far, but since there was no escape from that strong hand, told John of Mariel's scheme to race with George Barton. John groaned, but he did not slacken his hold until he had all the details of the race.

"Yes!" Sir Percy said vindictively, brushing down his wrinkled sleeve with a shaking hand, "I imagine they are even now setting out for Warlingham! A nice pastime for a well-bred young lady, is it not?"

John turned away abruptly, for there was no time to lose, saying over his shoulder as he opened the door, "I had better not hear that this has come to anyone else's ears, sir! I can assure you I would not hesitate to make you extremely uncomfortable in that case!"

Sir Percival bristled again. "You may count on my discretion, sir! I am sure I have no desire to discuss such a sordid bit of business! Besides," he added loftily, "I have only sincere sympathy for anyone who has the misfortune to be acquainted with the young lady!"

But he spoke to an empty doorway, for John had left and was rapidly making his way back to his rooms. He sent his man to order his curricle brought round at once and stripped off his elegant morning dress and attired himself in buckskin breeches and boots, thrusting a loaded pistol into one pocket of his many-caped driving coat, muttering to himself as he did so. By the time he had written a short note to Algy and charged his man to deliver it at once, the curricle was at the door, and he hastened out, leapt up to his seat, told the groom to let 'em go, and was off in a swirl of dust, the groom hopping nimbly up behind.

Mariel was indeed on her way to Warlingham. She had spent a great deal of time looking over both teams before deciding on a pair of grays. They were not much better than the roans she left for Barton, but they looked to be strengthy beasts, and not at all skittish. Barton congratulated her on her choice, and on the stroke of eleven, she tooled them out the gateway of the posting house and turned on the road south, an apprehensive Annie clutching her hat with one hand and the seat with the other. There was really no need for such caution, however, for it was a slow pace at first until they cleared the London streets, and Mariel was fretful that Barton would catch them up before she even reached the open road. First there was a large dray across the road backing into an alley that she had to pull up for and then a farm cart that had been upset by a young blood's carriage to negotiate around. She sighed with relief when she saw the countryside finally ahead of her, and she was able to urge her team to a faster pace. She was beginning to feel she was still well in the lead, when Barton's curricle overtook them and passed, that gentleman waving his whip in salute as he did so.

Mariel bit her lip in vexation. Now she was for it! She used her own whip, and the team picked up their pace a bit, allowing her to keep Barton in sight most of the time.

"Do not worry, Annie!" she said firmly. "He has sprung his horses too soon, and, when they begin to tire from the pace he has set, we will catch him easily!"

Annie was too busy hanging on and praying to reply.

Meanwhile, John was close behind, and since he kept excellent horses—regular sweet goers, fast as lightning—as his groom so often bragged to all his acquaintance—he soon came up on Mariel and passed her in a cloud of dust. Halting his horses, he turned them so they blocked the road, and sat and waited.

Mariel was forced to pull up, and she looked furiously to see who this might be and had the shock of seeing her friend John positively glaring at her.

"John! For the love of heaven, get out of the way! You will make me lose the race!" she cried as Annie clutched her arm and said, "Oh lordy, m'lady! Never speak so!"

John handed the reins to his groom and stepped down from his rig, and, maddeningly slow, approached the rented curricle. His face was so taut with anger,

anger such as she had never seen him exhibit before, that Mariel fell silent.

"The race, Mariel," he said between gritted teeth, "is over! Are you dead to all shame? How dare you behave in such a ramshackle manner? To make a wager with a known rake, for a contest no decent, well-brought-up young lady would ever agree to! You are lucky that news of this disgraceful to-do ever came to my ears this morning, or your reputation would be in shreds and tatters by nightfall! Yes, and your mother's and all the Carletons' as well! Is this how you repay their kindness?"

Mariel would have replied, but he was not finished in the slightest and continued rapidly, "You have run your course, Mariel! All your other escapades pale in comparison! What is your gauche conduct at an evening reception or walking down St. James Street when it is put beside such—such ill-mannered, shocking, *brazen* behavior as this? BAH!"

He finally paused for breath, and Mariel said in a conciliatory way, "But John, indeed I did not think it so bad, for I have my maid with me, and no one will know! Why, if you had not stopped me, I am sure I could have made Warlingham and beaten Mr. Barton as well, and been back in town long before dark!"

John laughed bitterly. "Oh yes, and Barton of course would be so good as to remain reticent about it, too! Or Sir Percival Rothsbottom from whom I learned of it this morning! You have so endeared yourself to *him* that of course he would not feel any need to regale the ton with an account of today's events! What a greenhorn you are, Mariel, thinking yourself awake on every suit, and well above the mores and strictures of society! For of course, what Lady Mary Ellen Winship does must always be admired!"

Mariel lowered her eyes at his sarcasm, and he put

his hands on his hips and added, "Although, to be sure, London has not seen *your* like before!"

He seemed to have run down, and Mariel put her hands to her hot face while Annie burst into tears beside her. To think that John—her good friend, John—would speak to her so!

"But—but what can I do, John? I must go on to Warlingham and admit I lost the race! Although," she added darkly, "it is all your fault that I did!"

She saw John's face become even more alarmingly red and was aware of the groom's interested gaze and Annie's anguished sobs, so she added hastily, "But I see we must not talk of that now! If I am at fault, I beg your pardon!"

Not a bit reassured by these placating words, John ignored her and pointed to Annie, still weeping gustily into her handkerchief.

"You there, girl! Whatever is the matter with you?"

Mariel leapt to her defense. "You have frightened her, John, and it is not her fault!"

"I am sure it is not," John agreed quickly. "The fault is all yours! Here, stop that weeping, girl, and get down. Madson will drive you home in my curricle, and I will return with Lady Mary Ellen to town. I find I have a great deal more to say to her!"

Annie sniffed and was heard to whisper she would so much rather not, but John strode to her side of the curricle and stretched up an imperious hand.

"Down! At once!"

"Oh sir," Annie wailed as she allowed him to help her down and transfer her to his own rig, "how can I go home without m'lady? Lady Carleton and Lady Winship are sure to ask where she is, and I—I know I will be blamed!"

John ignored her, and after he had given his groom orders, he strode back to Mariel.

"Move over, Lady Mary Ellen!" he said, and she was forced to comply as he stepped up into the curricle and took the reins from her hands. Meanwhile, Madson was turning John's pair and was soon heading back to town, a still weeping Annie beside him. His face was properly expressionless, but Mariel blushed when she saw how he stared at her as they passed.

John gave the grays the office to start, but he did not turn them and follow the other team.

"Where—where are we going?" Mariel asked in confusion.

"I have decided that we shall continue on to Warlingham! I find I have a great many things to discuss with George Barton, and it is only fair that we complete the course and put his mind to rest about your whereabouts. Yes, I have many things to tell him and they cannot wait!"

He whipped up the team, and they were soon tooling along much faster than Mariel had dared to drive. She would have spoken, but a sideways glance at John showed him still tight-lipped with rage, so she wisely desisted. An occasional word was heard from him, not at all complimentary, but all might have been well if Mariel had not heard him calling her a saucy, bold chit!

At that, her temper exploded.

"I am sure I do not know why you are so angry, to call me such a thing! Besides, you are not even related to me, so why is anything I do any business of yours?"

"Heaven protect me from all idiots!" John retorted, and whipped up the team as if he wished he had Mariel under the lash instead of the frightened grays. "What my future wife does is of course my business!"

"Your *wife?* Oh no!" Mariel exclaimed, vastly shocked.

John tightened his lips at her tone of disbelief and cracked his whip again.

"Oh, do be careful!" Mariel found herself saying. "I

am sure you should not drive so fast! Why, even the duke would not..."

John was furious that she compared him with his rival and did not slow the team. As they were even then approaching a narrow bridge, Mariel closed her eyes in horror and grasped the side of the seat more firmly.

There was an ominous cracking sound as the roadside wheel connected with the stone wall of the bridge, and then the team, slowed abruptly by the contact and frightened by the noise, panicked and bolted. John tried desperately to control them, but it was far too late, and the grays dragged them some distance before the damaged wheel came off and the curricle collapsed and tumbled across the road and down a grassy bank and settled on its side in a ditch.

Mariel lost consciousness for a minute and, when she came to, found herself in a heap on top of John. Blushing furiously, she extricated herself from the tangle, and then she gingerly moved her arms and legs. She was relieved that nothing seemed to be broken, although her head was throbbing in a horrid way. She put up a hand and was glad to find there was no blood, just a large bump that was even then beginning to swell. She crawled back to John who was, for the first time that morning, strangely silent. Mariel stared down in horror at his handsome, still white face.

"John! Oh John! Wake up!" she cried, but he did not respond. The curricle was still being jerked about by the team, now hopelessly tangled in the traces. The leader was down, and she was suddenly aware of his agonized screaming. "Oh John, wake up, do! I need you!" she implored, and as if in answer to her plea, he opened his eyes and stared at her. When he tried to move, he groaned, and then he put his left hand up to his shoulder and turned very pale.

"Oh dear, you are badly hurt!" Mariel exclaimed. "Quickly, give me your pistol!"

His mind whirling, and in the most excruciating pain he had ever known, John had a moment of stark terror. Surely he was not that badly off that even Mariel would contemplate shooting him to put him out of his misery! Then he heard the horse screaming and knew what she meant to do. He put out his hand and said weakly, "No, you cannot do it! I will!"

Mariel gave a rather shaky chuckle. "You cannot, John, please do not try to move! You might injure yourself far worse if you do! I assure you I will do it as quickly and as well as you could yourself, and I will be back to attend to you as soon as possible!"

John did not try to deter her anymore and pointed weakly to his greatcoat pocket. She reached in gingerly, trying not to jar him, and soon had the pistol in her hand. He heard her checking it, as if from a great distance, to make sure it was properly loaded and wished he had the strength to tell her that John Greeton never traveled with an unloaded weapon, but before he could speak, she was gone.

For a long moment he lay there, listening to the horse screaming, and feeling the bucking and pitching of the curricle which added so tremendously to his own agony, and then, just before he fainted, he heard the shot. He was not conscious long enough to know she had done it cleanly and as quickly reached out for the halter of the remaining horse to hold him steady when he would have bolted from fright if he could. It took a great deal of strength, wiry strength that no one would have suspected she possessed, seeing her in a dainty ballgown, or arranging flowers in the Carleton drawing room.

Mariel stayed with the horse until he was calm, and then she released him from the traces and led him a little distance away where she tied him to a branch. She tried not to look at the other horse, now mercifully silent, for although she had seen her Uncle James put animals out of their misery, she had never had to do it herself, and she had not realized that it would make her feel so queasy. She was shaking a little as she leaned against the flank of the gray, and then she put up her chin and moved swiftly back to the shattered curricle. This was no time for maidenly qualms or sensibilities, not with John lying injured and in shock. She must see to him and get help! But oh, for a moment she wished she might indulge in a fit of hysterics even though she knew such weakness would benefit nobody, least of all herself. She climbed down into the ditch to the now quiet curricle, realizing that her smart driving dress that had cost her mother so much money was most certainly ruined.

She found John stretched out on his side, his bad side, she saw with a sinking heart. He was such a big man, she wondered if she would have the strength to turn him over. He was unconscious again, and she knew the best time to see to him was now, when he was still senseless, and the pain of what she might have to do was not unbearable. She took a deep breath, grasped him by his good shoulder, and tried to turn him over onto his back. To her chagrin, she could not move him, and she sank back on her heels to consider the problem. She looked up briefly at the heavy clouds overhead and said a small prayer, and then she put one booted foot against his hip and pulled with all her might on his shoulder. All of a sudden, he tumbled over onto his back, and she fell backward herself into a very undignified position, her knees over her head. For some reason, it made her feel better, and she found herself laughing as she regained her feet.

Back at Greeton's side, she unbuttoned his coat and

took it off, not without a great deal of pulling to get it out from under him, and then she unbuttoned his shirt, no longer snowy white and immaculate. Carefully she felt down his right arm and gave a gasp when she realized it was severely broken. His legs in the tight buckskins appeared to be all right, but remembering how he had put his hand to his shoulder, she felt around his neck. As gentle as she tried to be, he moaned, and it was perfectly obvious to her probing fingers that he had also broken his collarbone.

For a moment she stayed still, her head bent and her breathing shallow as she contemplated what she should do now. She had never set a broken bone and thought she might do more damage than good if she tried, but she knew that the arm must be immobilized somehow until a doctor could see to him, and that as soon as possible! Taking a deep breath, she straightened out the broken arm as gently as she could and brought it up against his chest. Looking around for something to use as a sling, she wished she had thought to bring a shawl, but there was nothing that handy she could use. John moaned again and stirred, and hurriedly she removed her petticoat and tore off the bottom foot of it. She wrapped it around John's arm and, bringing the ends up around his neck, tied it securely. There! Unable to think of anything else to do after she had covered him with his greatcoat, she sat down beside him, her forehead damp with perspiration from her efforts. Now, Mariel, she told herself fiercely, so far so good, but what do you do now? You should not leave him, but he needs help soon, before it begins to rain! She glanced at the remaining horse, now grazing peacefully on the grassy verge. If she could get John up on the horse, she might be able to lead him to the next village, but that was clearly impossible. She didn't have the strength to put such a tall man up, and even if he could help her, she could not be sure he would not fall off in a moment of weakness and further injure himself. And why did no one come by, she asked herself in righteous indignation? Surely it was not too much to ask to expect a fellow traveler or a farmhand who might be of assistance! She looked eagerly up and down the road, but it remained empty. As she was considering riding the horse herself to get help, John stirred and moaned again. She bent over him anxiously, and he opened his eyes and looked up at her.

"Thank heavens!" he said weakly. "I would not have put it past you to shoot *me* to put me out of my misery!"

At that, Mariel burst into tears.

John stared at her perplexed, for he had never imagined she would dissolve in tears at such a little quip, and then he realized that all was quiet, the curricle was still, and he was lying stretched out on his back with his arm in a sling and warmly covered with his coat, and the pain was now a dull ache compared to the exquisite agony he had felt before. He drew a cautious breath and said, "My compliments, Mariel! I know of no women—and few men—who could have done so well!"

"That is quite the nicest thing anyone has ever said to me! Thank you!" she replied in naive gratitude, glad to put his absurd declaration of marriage right out of her mind, and hoping that he had forgotten it as well. "But what are we to do now? You cannot remain here; I must get you to shelter as soon as possible, for it looks distinctly like rain!" Eyeing the dark clouds overhead again, she continued, "I do not think you can ride in your condition. Do you have any idea where we are? Perhaps the best thing for me to do is ride for help...."

"In that gown? Bareback?" John asked incredulously. Before Mariel could reply and ruin the rapport between them, he said, "Let me see. We came through

Welton about noon. The next village is Merley, seven miles from Welton. Oh my head! Tell me, Mariel, did we come over a humpbacked bridge before we crashed? I cannot remember!"

Mariel thought hard. "Yes, yes we did! It was about a mile back, and I remember it because I was sure we were going to come to grief there, it was so narrow!"

John wisely decided to ignore this aspersion on his driving skill in view of their present predicament. "Then we are about three miles from Merley. There is a small inn there as I recall, and someone can be sent to fetch the doctor. But stay! Are you sure you are really all right? If you are hurt, I shall never forgive myself!"

Mariel felt a pang of pleasure that he should be so concerned for her and she replied quickly, "I am not injured, John. A bit bruised and dirty, and the gown is ruined, but no, not hurt!"

He sighed in relief. "Then, Mariel, if you would be so kind as to help me to my feet, I suggest we set out for Merley at once!"

"Walk to Merley? You cannot be serious! By your own reckoning it is three miles, and you so badly hurt! I must tell you I fear you have broken your collarbone as well as your arm!"

"I am not a fop or a helpless Corinthian!" John retorted. "Of course I can make Merley—there is nothing wrong with my legs!"

Mariel swallowed and said persuasively, "Let me walk to Merley! I can go much more quickly, and have help back that much sooner!"

"Perhaps," John frowned, "but it might take you awhile to convince the locals that you are a respectable female—ha! I hope you are a good actress, for I know I shall never see the day!" Mariel looked indignant and he continued, "By the by, do you know you have a black eye forming, as well as a most spectacular bump on your forehead? And that your gown is ripped and filthy? And even if you could convince them, it would take a while to harness up a team and wagon. No, just thinking about the jolting I would get on a hard farm wagon bed decides me! Thank you, I would rather walk!"

Much struck by this sentiment, for she had once been brought home in a farm cart herself when she had fallen off her mare and broken her wrist, Mariel could not help but agree. Silently she knelt and slid an arm under John's shoulders and helped him to sit up. He paused for a moment, leaning against her and breathing heavily, and then he said weakly, "Do me the kindness to find the flask in my greatcoat pocket! A little brandy and I shall do very well!"

Seeing his white, pale face, Mariel quickly found the flask and, opening it, held it to his lips. She saw his color improve after a long swallow, and he said in a more normal tone of voice, "Is there nothing I can use for support? That way I can help you more, for you will never be able to bear all my weight."

Mariel looked around, and spying one of the shafts from the curricle lying some little distance away, she got up and fetched it. It had snapped in two and was almost the perfect length to serve as a crutch.

It seemed to take forever, but in reality it was only a few minutes before John was on his feet and leaning on the shaft while Mariel hurried to bring the horse closer.

And so, the two young people—one in a dirty torn gown minus her petticoat, with a black eye, bruises, and bumps, and the other with his good hand thrust through the gray's halter and his broken arm and collarbone aching ferociously again—began their walk to Merley.

TEN

It would be pleasant to be able to report that the journey was passed in perfect amity, with each helping the other in true Christian fellowship, but such was not the case.

They had not traveled very far before they began to bicker, each roundly condemning the other for the predicament they were in. Mariel had to admit that it was her foolhardiness that led them to the beginning of the adventure, but was not slow to point out that if John had been the kind of driver the duke was, the accident would never have happened. This comparison so infuriated him that John rang a mighty peal over her. Truth be told, he was worried about Mariel's plight, alone with a man who was not even a relative, and he was sorry he had ever mentioned his wish to marry her. Gloomily, he decided she would have to accept him now, whether she wanted to or not, since he had ruined her reputation. These thoughts, and the pain he was in, made it difficult to be civil.

Fortunately, they were both so soon out of breath from their exertions that all recriminations ceased. When they stopped for a moment by mutual consent, John leaned heavily against the horse who looked around in mild curiosity, while Mariel tried to ignore her aching head and twitched the halter impatiently.

"How far do you think we have come, sir?" she asked distantly. "Surely we must be almost to the village by now!"

It was only by the severest strength of will that John was keeping himself from fainting, for he knew that if he did so, he would be unable to rise, even with Mariel's help.

"If we have come a mile I would be surprised!" he answered shortly. "Try not to be so silly! I thought you were a country woman!"

Mariel's eyes widened in shock. How dare he insult her when she was trying as hard as she could to help him! Before she could reply, he added impatiently, "Come! Let us be on our way!"

Obediently, she led the horse forward, trying to go as slowly as possible. As they moved off, she could not help saying tartly over her shoulder, "What a shame that it is not Miss Wiltwick or Lady Aston-Byley who is here with you, Mr. Greeton! Even though they are not 'countrywomen,' I am sure their help would be vastly more acceptable to you!"

John chuckled weakly. "They would be of absolutely no use at all! Have your wits gone begging? Miss Wiltwick would have hysterics and call for her mama, and Lady Aston-Byley would never stop bemoaning the loss of her gown and the lack of an audience for her heroics!"

Mariel could not help smiling a little at his description even as she added, in a shocked tone, "But John! They are the leading beauties! The Incomparables of the London scene!"

"They are only incomparable in a very limited setting! Take 'em out of the ballroom, and what have you got?"

This rhetorical question went unanswered, for just then he stumbled on a loose stone, and groaned as the broken bones were jarred. Mariel would have continued the conversation for it helped her to forget her aches and bruises, but in no uncertain terms John told her to be quiet.

"I cannot attend to you now, Mariel! I have seldom felt less like polite conversation! Cut line!"

At that, Mariel put up her chin and determined that no matter what happened, she would preserve a silent dignity from then on. She found it hard to believe that he had mentioned marriage only a short while ago, and now he was being positively rude! Surely she had not heard him correctly!

And so, much later, they came at last to Merley, for John was in such pain they had had to stop a number of times. By the time they had straggled up the street to the inn, they had attracted quite an audience. There were several children, a number of mongrel dogs all barking at them, and a farmhand who seemed to feel they were part of some wonderful raree-show, come to Merley to entertain the populace. He kept pointing to them and laughing, until Mariel lost her temper and told him to be off! It was really too much, she thought darkly, and if she did not sit down soon and rest, she would have a bout of hysterics the likes of which would have had Miss Wiltwick stunned in admiration!

John called as loudly as he could for the landlord, but when Mr. Holland appeared at the door of the inn, he stopped dead and stared at them, his broad welcom-

144

ing smile fading as his mouth fell open and the towel he was holding dropping unheeded to the ground.

"Here, man, help me in!" John growled. "Is Merley populated only by idiots? Can't you see we—my cousin and I, I mean—have had an accident and require a doctor at once?"

Mariel silently applauded this quick thinking as Mr. Holland moved forward quickly. Dirty and disheveled they might be, but he knew the quality, even though they rarely stopped at the Lamb and Lion. Never mind the lady's dirty face and black eye, or the gentleman's lacy sling, his tone of voice said they were no ordinary travelers! Mr. Holland called for a stablehand to take the tired gray, and John gladly transferred his weight to the landlord's broad shoulders. By this time Mrs. Holland had arrived, along with a small maid, and taking in the situation at a glance said sharply, "You, Fred! When you have stabled the horse, take the gig to fetch the doctor! Lizzie, upstairs and make the best bedrooms ready at once, and send Meg for hot water and bandages!"

Mariel sighed in relief as she was led into the inn, much to the disappointment of the village children and the crowd the farmhand had called up to see the show.

With some difficulty, John was helped up the narrow stairs and into a front bedroom. The landlord took his coat gently and proceeded to help him undress, after which he put him between the sheets in one of his own nightshirts. John sighed as his head came to rest on the pillows and after another sip of brandy said he would do very well until the doctor arrived. Mr. Holland would have liked to ask the young gentleman who he was and what had happened, but he saw that John was dropping off into a restless sleep and was not sorry when Mariel came in and said she would sit with her cousin until the doctor came. She asked Mr. Holland about this worthy and his skill and, when she found out he was often called to the Hall, and was quite a favorite with the squire's lady, relaxed, for she wanted no local horse doctor touching John and making things worse. She had had time to remove her bonnet and brush some of the dirt from her gown while the landlady brought a towel and some hot water, and felt a great deal better after she had washed her face and hands. But when she saw her eye and the bump on her forehead, she was much shocked. Mrs. Holland promised to bring her a hot cup of tea directly, and she gave up bemoaning her appearance in the old wavy mirror over the mantel in her bedroom and hurried to John's side.

She would have felt Mr. Holland impertinent when he began to question her closely if she had not seen how badly they both looked, so she went out of her way to reassure him.

"Someone must be sent to London immediately," she said as grandly as she could. "My cousin and I will be missed, for we were only on a visit to relatives in Warlingham and were due to return before dark!"

On the landlord's pointing out what Warlingham was closer and it would be quicker to notify her relatives there, she stumbled a little and finally declared that word must be sent to London, "for we were not expected in Warlingham, and meant to surprise Aunt Bess!"

The landlord bowed and left her, saying to himself as he went down the stairs, "Aye, Missie, that's what *you* say, but what *I* say is there's something haveycavey about all this!" He hurried to the kitchen to confer with his wife, not at all sure they had done the right thing taking such a pair in, for he had no desire to get tangled up in the elopement which he strongly began to suspect was the present case.

Gratefully Mariel drank her tea and ate the bread and butter the maid brought, watching John toss his head fitfully on the pillows. She had never realized how handsome he was, she thought, as she stared at his strong features and well-cut mouth and spent several moments pondering the one statement he had made that day that would not leave her mind. Could he have meant it? Marriage? To her? John groaned in his sleep, and she hoped the doctor would not be long in arriving. Soon thereafter, she heard a rig pull up to the inn door, and she hurried to the window and peered out. She could not see who it might be, but she recognized the voice that drifted up the stairwell and went quickly to the door.

"Oh, Mr. Barton, how glad I am to see you! Do come up!" she implored.

Barton handed his hat to the landlord, his eyes widening as he stared up at her.

"Good gad, Lady Mary Ellen! What has happened? I waited for you at Warlingham, and when it grew later and later, I made my way back, hoping to find some clue. I had almost concluded you had given up and returned to town!"

Mariel colored up. "Of course I did not!" she snapped as he came lightly up the stairs. "John Greeton caught me up and insisted on driving the curricle! He sent my maid back to town with his groom, and then..." Suddenly conscious of the interested audience below, hanging on her every word, she stopped and opened the door to John's room.

"Won't you come in, sir? I shall be glad to tell you all about it when we are more private!"

Barton followed her in, and she shut the door with a snap. He had been stunned when he saw her eye and the swelling on her forehead, but now he was with Greeton, lying completely still in an old four-poster, he felt a flickering of alarm. There would be a great scandal if the boy died, and it would all be laid at his door.

"Is he . . . is he *dead?*" he asked in a shocked whisper.

"Of course not!" Mariel replied stoutly. "He has broken his collarbone and his right arm rather badly, but he is only asleep now! I suspect it was the walk to the inn and the brandy he has been sipping against the pain that lets him lie so quietly!"

Much relieved, Barton took a chair near hers and was soon told everything that had happened since he had passed her on the road. He said everything that was proper, and soon had Mariel feeling much calmer now she did not have to face the consequences alone.

When the doctor arrived, he put them both out, saying brusquely that he would do very well with only Mr. Holland's help and later would see to the young lady whom he advised to go and lie down on her bed. Mariel was glad to be banished, for she did not at all like the look of the instruments in his case. She retired to her room, leaving a subdued Barton to go down to the taproom for a pint and some serious thinking.

He was summoned back to John's room some time later when the doctor was closeted with Mariel. Strolling in, Barton was pleased to see him awake, lying propped up on the pillows with his arm encased in a much more professional-looking sling.

"I have asked to see you, Barton," John began grimly, "before they give me any laudanum to make me sleep!"

"Behold me in attendance, sir! May I say I am delighted that you took no serious hurt?"

John snorted, for the past half hour had been very hard to bear. Pointing his good hand at Barton, he said, "I shall have something more to say to you, sir, when I am feeling more the thing, for leading the Lady Mary Ellen into such a scrape!"

"Oh, but it was not so bad, surely? Indeed, the lady was most eager to race; I did but mention it in jest before she took me up in earnest—much to my surprise!" Barton said easily, not at all reluctant to castigate Mariel, and then he added archly, "I am sure she did it to impress Algy, you know!"

John stared at him. "Whyever would she want to do that?" he asked in a voice of complete incomprehension.

"Why, since it is such a case with them!" Barton replied, and then as John continued to stare, he added, "I do hope he will not feel he has to offer for the girl immediately! As his friends we must keep him from rushing his fences, don't you agree? To plunge into marriage with such a hoyden even though he thinks himself too deep in love..."

"ALGY marry MARIEL?" John interrupted in astonishment. "You must be mad!"

"But my dear Greeton, do consider!" Barton said, feeling that John must be slightly deranged with pain. "He has been in love with her this age..."

"IN LOVE? WITH MARIEL? Have you been drinking, Barton? To Algy, she is a tiresome and annoying young relative, nothing more! *I* am the one who intends to marry her, not Algy!"

Barton sat down abruptly, his mind in a whirl. "But... but I thought—good heavens, he has given all the signs of a man in love, and it was only to protect him from his folly that I undertook to lure the lady away! If not Mariel, then who? Algy was forever in her company...." He looked up to catch John frowning and with such a mulish expression on his face that he knew that further questions would only go unanswered.

"Well, let us say no more about it!" he said easily. "I shall be glad to return to town and tell Lady Winship and the Carletons where you both are. Yes, perhaps that would be best! It will be midafternoon before I can reach them, and they will be worried!"

John agreed that this would be helpful, not understanding why Algy had not followed him immediately on receiving his note. His tone was so aloof and distant that Barton flushed a little, knowing that when Greeton told his tale, he would never again be any particular crony of Algernon Carleton and, shrugging his shoulders lightly in defeat, took his leave gracefully.

"Be sure and tell Lady Mary Ellen all that is polite, and my best wishes for your swift recovery! If I thought there was anything further I could undertake to assist you, I would..."

"No further assistance from you, Barton, is necessary!" John interrupted grimly. "Your part in this is over, and I would appreciate your reticence about it as well. But I am sure you will see that silence is the wisest course, for luring young girls to curricle races does not reflect very well on you!"

Barton bowed, completely silenced by John's tone of voice, and left him. He was soon on his way back to London, much regretting the rich pigeon who had escaped his snares, and dumbfounded that he had so mistaken Algy's feelings for the lady.

In the meantime, Mariel had been examined by the doctor, who pronounced her perfectly fit, although he chuckled a little as he said it, looking at her colorful eye. He left some ointment for her bumps and bruises and took himself off after promising to look in on John in the morning, who, he said, must on no account be moved.

Mariel missed Barton's departure, but she could only be glad when she learned of it from the landlord. His presence had made her feel very uncomfortable, perhaps because it reminded her of her part in the day's misfortunes. Besides, he would tell the Carletons and her mother where they were—and oh, she did begin to feel the need for her mother's support!

She was making her way down the narrow stairs to confer with Mrs. Holland about their dinner, when the inn door was thrown open and a gentleman stepped hurriedly inside. Mariel had time to see that it was raining now in earnest and threatened to continue to do so for some time. She was grateful that at least they had reached the inn before that was added to her troubles!

She came to the bottom of the stairs and would have passed the man with a distant nod, when she heard him speak in horrified tones. "Pon rep! It cannot be!"

Looking up she beheld Toddles Bellington retreating hurriedly from her vicinity, his eyes bulging with shock.

"Sir?" she asked, as aloofly as possible. "Were you addressing me?"

"No, no! Get back! Why do I have the misfortune to keep meeting you? For now I see you are here, it will be impossible for me to remain! What is a little rain after all when put up against the possible consequences that might occur to anyone in your neighborhood?"

Mariel drew herself up. "I assure you, sir," she said, "there is no need for such dramatics! I shall stay well out of your way!"

Mr. Bellington scowled at her and then, leaning closer, said, "Perhaps I would be safe after all, for I see you have already found a victim today! I am delighted that *HE* at least came out a winner!"

He cackled as Mariel looked at him in confusion until he pointed to her eye, but when she would have replied indignantly, he shook his head at her and sidled past to enter the taproom, muttering to himself. Mariel felt a distinct lump in her throat and hot tears beginning to form. What a horrible day it had turned out to be! She could imagine nothing worse happening, unless the inn burned down, and she would not be a bit surprised if it did!

She was wrong. The horrible day was in no way over.

Algy had spent the morning riding with friends and, in returning late to his rooms, found John's note and was much puzzled by it. Because of his haste, John had only written that he was following Mariel and George Barton to Warlingham, and promised to return the lady to London as soon as possible. He suggested that Algy might care to ride out and meet them. Algy was confused. If John had indeed chased Mariel to Warlingham, they must be well on their way home by now. He shook his head over this latest start, for he was definitely at a loss as to why she was going there with Barton. Why Warlingham? It was not noted for any historic antiquities or pleasant walks or scenic picnic spots that he knew of, and even if they were friends, he could not approve her choice of companion for the venture!

Without changing out of his riding clothes, he went at once to St. James Square where he found that not only had Mariel not returned, but both his mother and his cousin were in a state of extreme agitation. While out shopping they had seen both the Misses Wiltwicks, who were obviously not entertaining at a luncheon and card party, and Lady Carleton had directed her coachman to return home at once, saying to Ellen in a voice of deep foreboding, "Yes, and I have known this age that she was about to do something truly outrageous for it has been some time since her last escapade! Oh dear, what can it be?"

Lady Winship was also worried, but she tried hard to remain calm. By the time Algy was announced, Annie had been summoned and questioned, and the whole story of the race had come out.

"But where can they be?" moaned Lady Carleton, after a weeping Annie had been dismissed. "Surely they have had time to get to Warlingham and back by now! I fear there has been some accident! That poor, poor young man! And when I think he went to save her from her folly!"

Algy tried futilely to calm both ladies, and while they were still discussing the incident, Ridgeway announced a Mr. George Barton. When Lady Carleton would have denied him, the butler coughed and added that the gentleman said he had news of Lady Mary Ellen and Mr. Greeton, and his mistress snapped at him, "Send him in at once, Ridgeway! Why do you stand there with that look on your face? But stay!"—as he turned to leave with slow measured steps—"I am not at home to anyone else who might call! It is the outside of enough to be polite to everyone in town right now!"

She took up her salts and handkerchief again as Ridgeway bowed and went to escort Mr. Barton to the salon.

The story was soon told, and after he had left them, rather hurriedly since both ladies had stared at him so unpleasantly when they learned of his part in the race, and young Carleton had refused to acknowledge him in any way, Algy began to berate his erstwhile friend all the while offering to escort them both to the inn at Merley.

"Thank you, Algy, that would be most kind of you!" Lady Winship said with a smile.

"Why, oh why, is your father not here?" moaned Lady Carleton. "But that is the trouble with men! Never around when you need 'em, but constantly underfoot when you don't!"

The carriage was ordered for an hour later to allow everyone to pack such clothes and necessities as they thought they might require. Algy hurried away to collect a valise for John as well, and Annie was informed that she was to have the treat of accompanying the ladies and traveling yet again the road to Warlingham. Resigned, she went to pack a portmanteau for Lady Mariel.

By half past four they were on their way, only slightly delayed by Lady Carleton's insisting on bringing a large case of such remedies as might benefit John, including jars of calf's foot jelly and other restoratives, as well as ointments and potions for every disease known to man. Algy impatiently pointed out that Merley was hardly located in a wilderness surrounded by savage natives, and by Barton's own account, a doctor had already seen both John and Mariel, but she ignored him. Lady Winship was very quiet, but he could tell by her hands, endlessly twisting a handkerchief, that she was far from calm, and he wished one more time that he had the right to put his arms around her and comfort her. Instead, he undertook to distract both ladies with light conversation while Annie huddled in her corner, quiet as a mouse, with only an occasional sniffle escaping her.

Algy's efforts were only partially successful, for Lady Carleton continued to refer to the race and the accident, and to speculate on what had caused it and why young Greeton had not returned to London immediately. When it began to rain, their progress was necessarily slowed, to everyone's chagrin, and the trip began to seem endless before they reached Merley and the Lamb and Lion.

Algy helped the ladies down and into the inn where they found the landlord hurrying out of the taproom to greet his new guests. "Well, it's an ill wind..." he thought to himself gleefully, rubbing his hands together at the thought of entertaining such members of the quality. He escorted the ladies upstairs, Annie following with the heavy bag of remedies, and Algy stayed below to see that their bags were brought in and rooms prepared before strolling to the taproom until the initial fuss and flurry should be over.

He was surprised to find Toddles Bellington before the fire. Mr. Bellington knew him slightly and was delighted to have an audience to tell of his unfortunate meeting with that young person again, and what he had said to her, the chit! Algy did not encourage him; in fact he mentioned solemnly that the young lady's mother had just arrived and would be most upset to find her daughter's name being bandied about a common taproom. This information had the effect of reducing Mr. Bellington to a few quiet grumbles as Algy took off his wet coat and called for some wine. He was forced to smile grimly a little as he thought of Mariel's meeting with Toddles. Really, she did have the most appalling luck, almost as if the fairy in attendance at her birth had decided that freckles and red hair were not enough of a disadvantage!

A short time later, reassured that John was comfortably asleep and had taken no permanent harm, Lady Carleton went to the private parlor that had been engaged for them all, and it was here that she and Algy first saw Mariel as she came in with her mother. Algy, who had stored up a number of cutting things to say to her was struck speechless, and even Lady Carleton dropped her reticule and stared.

"Good God, Mariel! Whatever have you done—and I thought freckles were—oh dear! You will have to leave town now—it is turning purple—so awful with your hair!"

Mariel sniffed. She had thrown herself into her mother's arms and surrendered to the tears she had been holding back all afternoon, and wisely Lady Winship had not scolded her, but just hugged her until she was calm. She had tried to avoid Lady Carleton, for she would have preferred to go directly to bed now her mother was here, but Lady Winship had insisted she come and apologize. Now she took a deep breath and said, "I cannot tell you how sorry I am, Aunt Daphne, that this has happened! But John insisted on driving!"

Lady Carleton looked confused. "But of course—quite right that he should! Oh, do go and get to bed! We can talk in the morning! Perhaps I have some ointment that would help that eye—but not cream of strawberry this time!" she chuckled.

Mariel said the doctor had left her everything she required and would have taken her leave of them all when a knock came at the door and Algy opened it to disclose the Duke of Chatham.

The duke had called in St. James Square shortly after the carriage had left for Merley and would have left his card and departed on learning that the ladies were out, when Ridgeway said in a curiously expressionless voice, "Yes, Your Grace, I believe they are even now on their way to Merley with Mr. Algy to join the Lady Mary Ellen and Mr. Greeton."

The duke stared at him, one black eyebrow raised in inquiry.

"To Merley? Why are Lady Mariel and young Greeton there?"

Ridgeway sniffed disapprovingly, although it was obvious he was big with news. "I am sure I cannot say, Your Grace," and then catching sight of the handsome *pourboire* the duke was fingering, he added, "I believe there has been a curricle accident in which the young people were involved, and Lady Winship, supported by her aunt, is hurrying to their sides!"

The duke lounged against a hall table. "If there was an accident, it goes without saying that Lady Mary Ellen was involved! Are they badly hurt?"

"No, I believe not, according to a Mr. Barton who called with the news. Mr. Greeton has sustained a broken arm, and the lady some bruises. She shot the horse." Ridgeway sniffed again.

"Shot the horse? What has that to say to anything?" the duke asked, and when Ridgeway would have explained, he waved his hand and said easily, "Thank you, you have told me quite enough!"

Handing the butler the guinea, he made his way home in deep thought. Damn Mariel to upset her mother again, he thought grimly as he changed his clothes and called for his racing curricle. He informed his man that he was leaving to meet friends, and would expect him at Chatham Park in three days unless he sent other word.

"Very good, Your Grace," that excellent manservant said, calmly packing a cloak bag for him, and not at all concerned that his master was setting out in the rain so late in the day.

Now the duke stood dripping in the doorway of the private parlor and surveyed them all, but his eyes went first to Lady Winship, a fact not missed by her aunt. He thought she looked tired and distraught and longed to comfort her, and it was with an effort that he turned to Mariel. The sight of her woebegone face with its bump and colorful swollen eye did much to stem his anger at her, but he merely nodded and said, "Just what you deserve! I could not have thought of a better punishment, although my dear Mariel, you should by all rights be whipped as well! Indeed, I wish I might have the schooling of you, if only for a short while!"

He strolled over and took her chin in one strong hand and turned her face to the light, as Lady Winship said quickly, "Your Grace! Whatever are you doing here? How did you know?"

Lady Carleton moaned again and waved her salts.

"Do not, my dear Chatham, tell me it is all over town in such a short time! How very mortifying!"

"No, m'lady," he smiled at them both. "I heard it from your own butler after I questioned him most particularly, and I came to offer you my support!"

Lady Carleton did not seem to find anything amiss in this statement, and Lady Winship smiled in gratitude as the duke dropped Mariel's chin and said carelessly, "You should be in bed, child! I am sure we will all be able to contain our disappointment that you must leave us!"

Mariel tried to smile at him. "Indeed, Your Grace, it was not my fault! You are not to think I have profited so little from your lessons! If John had not insisted on driving when he was so angry with me, he would not have handled the team as badly as Algy is wont to do, and we would never have come to grief on that narrow bridge, but there was no reasoning with him, and..."

"Yes, yes, we will hear all about it tomorrow! Off with you now, at once!" the duke said sternly, as Algy colored up and ground one fist against the other at Mariel's insult.

Seeing his furious face, Mariel curtseyed quickly and fled, but when Lady Winship would have followed her, the duke stopped her and said, smiling down at her gently, "She will do very well by herself, Lady Winship, and feel much better after a good night's rest. Come and sit down by the fire; you look done up, and I want you to drink a glass of wine!"

As he led her to a chair, Algy glanced up and saw his mother smiling and nodding, and wondered what on earth she had to look so pleased about, especially since that chit had just insulted her son so baldly!

The four of them sat down to dinner some time later. Algy and the duke had arranged to sit up with John in shifts through the night in case he should require something, and both ladies were glad to go to bed fairly early, so tired out from their exertions and the alarums of the day as they both were.

ELEVEN

Everyone but John slept late the following morning. He woke to the sound of heavy rain and for a moment could not remember where he was, but the pain in his arm and neck quickly recalled him to his circumstances, and he groaned. He seemed to remember Lady Carleton bending over him and, at one point during the long restless night, the Duke of Chatham, but he must have been dreaming, he told himself, for what would the duke be doing here, tucking in the cover he had thrown off in his restlessness and giving him a drink and telling him to go back to sleep? He looked around the bedroom, dim in the gray morning light, and was surprised to see Algy Carleton stretched out in an armchair fast asleep. How curious! When had he arrived from London, and why did he not sleep in a bed? That armchair looked very uncomfortable! He tried to move, and the pain washed over him again and he groaned even more loudly.

At the sound, Algy came awake, and rubbing a hand over his unshaven face, he rose and came to the bed.

"John? Are you awake?" he asked, watching his friend anxiously.

"Yes! But I wish I were not!" John retorted. "Oh, this shoulder!"

Algy looked at the clock on the mantel. "It is still too early for your next draught. Shall I call the maid and order some hot coffee? Or do you feel you can eat something? I have to warn you that my mother has brought all kinds of invalid foods and medicines; perhaps a spoonful of pork jelly would make you feel better?"

"Pork jelly?" John repeated in tones of disbelief. "I don't want any pork jelly, man! I want some ham or perhaps a slice of sirloin, some bread and cheese and eggs, a tankard of ale and several cups of coffee!"

Algy grinned at him. "I'll see what I can do, unless the doctor has left special orders for your feeding, but there'll be no ale for you today, not with all the laudanum you've been taking!"

He left the room before John had a chance to question him, so there was nothing to do but settle back on his pillows and sigh. He was dozing again when Algy returned, followed by a maid with a large tray containing several steaming dishes. Algy had taken the time to shave and change his clothes, and looked so much refreshed that John eyed him cynically and said thickly through a mouthful of ham, "Quite the dapper dog, ain't we? Did you think to bring my man, Algy? I could use a shave myself!"

"No, I left him in town. I felt the less people who knew about this, the better! So you will have to put up with my ministrations, and, oh yes, the Duke of

Chatham's. Perhaps you would rather be shaved by a member of the peerage?"

John frowned at him. "Whatever is he doing here? I was sure I was dreaming last night when I woke to find him!"

"He has come to support the ladies through this ordeal; I tell you John, I cannot see what the man sees in Mariel! It is a complete mystery why he still pursues her after all her scrapes!"

John scowled at this bit of news. So, the duke had come after Mariel, had he? His heart sank, then he roused himself from his contemplations and asked, "And how is Mariel today? She took no hurt from the accident, did she?"

Algy poured him some more coffee and cut up another slice of ham. "You are managing very well with your left hand, John! If it were I, I would be sure to have the bed littered with food! As for Mariel, I have not seen her this morning, but she went to bed last night with the most vivid black eye I have ever seen! No," he added truthfully, "not black! It was purple and green! My mother declared it gave her a twinge it was such a horrible color combination with her hair! But I say it was no more than she deserved, my dear, sweet, shy, *retiring* cousin!"

John choked a little over his coffee at Algy's acerbic tones, and then he leaned back replete, and Algy removed the tray from his knees. It was not long before he had the whole story of yesterday's adventure.

"How long am I to be kept in bed?" John asked impatiently as Algy straightened his pillows.

His friend admitted he had no idea but had heard the doctor would be calling today. "But you don't feel like getting up, surely?" he asked.

"Lord no! I feel terrible!"

Algy was assuring him he could soon have another

dose of medicine that would make him fall asleep, when Lady Carleton knocked and entered, followed by Annie and the bag of medicine. John looked at it askance as she bustled up to the bed and asked how he did. She began to unpack the bag, and John said quickly, "Now, Lady Carleton, please do not bother! I am sorry to be such a nuisance, but it is only broken bones after all, and not a wound or deathbed illness!"

"Besides," Algy added, "he has just eaten a huge breakfast and he hates pork jelly as much as I do!"

"You do? I was not aware you had ever had any!" Lady Carleton said calmly, ignoring both young men. "You will soon grow accustomed to it, John, for it is very good for you, you'll see! Besides, I feel I stand in your mother's place here, and there is nothing I would not do to help you recover after all you have done for Mariel. It was so kind of you to come to her aid!" She beamed at him fondly, but was finally persuaded to go away until John could be shaved and made more presentable, and when she came back some time later, it was to find him fast asleep in one of Algy's nightshirts, looking ridiculously young and boyish to her eyes.

She insisted Algy go down to the parlor and let her sit with his friend, so he took himself off, hoping to find Lady Winship. Find her he did, but not alone for she was with the duke in the parlor having breakfast. The duke did not look at all pleased this morning. Perhaps, Algy thought as he took a seat after reassuring Lady Winship that he had already eaten, he is tired out from his nursing duties. He inquired for Mariel and was told she was still asleep. Under the duke's questioning, Lady Winship told them as much as she knew of the accident, and Algy volunteered the information John had given him about it.

"So she did shoot the horse!" the duke said faintly. "What a redoubtable girl she is!"

"I am sure it was very brave of her," Lady Winship said. "But you must know she is used to animals, and she could never leave one in pain like that!"

"And then to help John all those miles to the inn!" Algy said in some surprise. "Why, looking at it that way, she is quite the heroine!"

The duke looked at him sharply. "I must beg you, dear boy, not to put that idea in her head! The longer she lives with the results of her folly in accepting Barton's challenge, and with our disapproval, the calmer life will be for us all! If she gets the idea she is noble and heroic, beware!"

Algy stated fervently that as far as he was concerned, she would *never* know it, and Lady Winship excused herself so she might go and look in on her daughter. As both men rose and bowed her out, they each wondered how anyone so calm and lovely could ever have produced Mariel!

It was not long before the doctor arrived, and he went at once to John's room where he pronounced himself satisfied with his patient's progress, although he told Lady Carleton and the duke that under no circumstances should the young man be moved, for any unnecessary jarring might disturb the healing. As he was leaving the inn, the duke questioned him in more detail, and finally wrung permission from him to move John to Chatham Park in a few days.

"My carriage is extremely well-sprung, and I am sure he will sustain no hurt," the duke said with calm authority. "And he will be so much more comfortable there where he can be well attended!" The doctor knew Chatham Park and agreed tentatively to the scheme, depending on John's rate of recovery and amount of pain.

John slept on and off the rest of the day, with various members of the party taking turns sitting with him.

Mariel rose very late, feeling better for her long sleep, but still very sore and bruised. She had not realized she had hurt her leg, but it ached this morning and caused her to limp slightly. As she brushed her hair and Annie helped her to dress, she avoided looking in the mirror, for, as she told the maid, "I look a perfect fright! Enough to scare small children if they should catch a glimpse of me!"

Annie giggled and had to agree with her. It was almost lunchtime when she made a hesitant appearance in the parlor, having sent Annie ahead to see if Toddles Bellington was anywhere in sight before she ventured from her room.

Her mother rose from a chair near the window where she had been reading a book of poetry and went to help her daughter as she limped in. Mariel greeted the duke and Algy in a hushed little voice that caused the duke to smile cynically.

"I hope you are feeling better, Mariel, after your great adventure?" he asked.

Algy frowned mightily at her and she flushed. "Thank you, Your Grace, much better although I am very sore. Perhaps the horse kicked me and I did not remember it in the excitement! And how is John—I mean Mr. Greeton, today? I thought I heard the doctor's voice awhile ago."

Algy told her John was still in some pain but sleeping most of the time, the best remedy of all. Mariel sighed and went to the window to stare out at the rain.

"What a dreary day!" she observed sadly.

"Yes!" Algy agreed. "And if it had only rained like this yesterday, your ridiculous wager would have been canceled, but alas, we were not so fortunate!"

"Hear, hear!" Chatham agreed heartily.

Lady Winship smiled at him. He was upset and disturbed by Mariel's actions, she knew, but the fact that he had come so quickly to be with her was an encouraging sign! Surely he must be in love if he could ignore her daughter's really horrible appearance! The eye was even more colorful today, and she made a note to ask Daphne how long such bruises lasted, for even the duke would hardly ask Mariel to marry him while she sported such colors! She did not mind his sarcasm when he spoke to Mariel; indeed it was less than she deserved, and she was sure that after their union, the duke would have no trouble controlling such a willful miss!

"Oh!" Mariel exclaimed from her post by the window, "there goes Mr. Bellington! I wonder he cares to travel in such a downpour!"

"I saw him paying his shot when I spoke to the doctor," the duke replied. "He told me that not even a flood could induce him to remain in a place where he was in such grave danger! But I am sure he exaggerated, at least a little!"

Mariel blushed painfully, and Algy took pity on her and asked if she would care to play cards. He had found an old pack in one of the table drawers, and the two of them were soon engrossed.

Lady Carleton joined them for luncheon, and Mariel insisted on taking a turn in the sickroom while her aunt rested.

"I am sure I would be glad for a rest, Mariel, but do not hesitate to call me if you need help. I am afraid he is a very bad patient, but perhaps it is because he is in such pain!"

Mariel promised she would do so if John proved troublesome and then said casually, not looking at anyone, that she believed that most men made very bad patients. She left the room to the heated denials of both the duke and Algy.

John was asleep when she entered softly, and after

she had adjusted one of the curtains so the light did not disturb him, she sat down to read. When he awoke, John had the pleasure of seeing her close to him, her red curls bent over her book. She seems to bring the sunshine in, he thought muzzily, and was content to gaze at her without speaking. Suddenly she looked up, and, when she saw that he was awake, she smiled and rose.

"Dear John!" she said fondly, causing his heart to race. "How do you do? Is there anything I can get for you? Some tea, perhaps?"

"No, no!" John said. "I want nothing! Just stay and talk to me!"

"Are you in pain?" she persisted. "Here, let me fluff up your pillows!" She bent over him, and he wished he was not hurt for then he could put his arms around her and tell her he had not meant to be so cross yesterday, even as he bit his lips and bore the inevitable jostling without a murmur. Even her colorful eye did not bother him, not with her lips so close! He closed his eyes, afraid he might say or do something to frighten her, and when he opened them again, she had moved away.

"But I do not understand!" Mariel teased him. "Lady Carleton said you were a bear, and here I find you are very good!"

John could have told her that her ministrations were much preferable to her aunt's, but he only replied while he continued to gaze longingly at her, his heart in his eyes, "The pain is nothing!"

Mariel was beginning to feel a little uncomfortable. Things had changed between the two of them, and now there were undercurrents that disturbed her. Taking a deep breath, and wishing she had her old friend back, she came closer to the bed and said shyly, "I must thank you, John, for coming so swiftly to my rescue! I have had a chance to think about the race...and...and I realize it was a very foolish thing to do! I know I have made a great deal of trouble for everyone, and most especially for you, and I know I do not deserve such kindness, even from such a good friend as you are!"

"A good friend?" John asked slowly. "Well, yes, of course I am that, but I hope..."

He might have continued to press his suit except Lady Winship came in just then, and the three of them talked together until the duke arrived to administer John's medicine.

"I think you had better retire, Lady Winship, Mariel!" he said cheerfully. "I have to move this young scamp, and he is not at all reticent about the fact that I am less than a trained attendant!"

John protested he was not so gauche, but the duke just smiled.

"Perhaps you do not remember what you said to me last night, Greeton, but I do! It made me well aware of all my shortcomings, and the language was such that no lady should hear. I will try to do better this time!"

He held the door open for Lady Winship after Mariel had passed through, a fond smile on his face and his gray eyes glowing as he looked down at her.

She blushed, wondering why her heart was beating so rapidly, as John called from the bed, "You will come back, Mariel, won't you? Indeed, I feel much better now!"

Mariel promised to return shortly, and Lady Winship went to her room for a moment alone to compose herself. Whatever is the matter with you, Ellen, she asked herself crossly. Remember that the duke is kind to you for Mariel's sake, and you are only imagining a warmer feeling! But oh, she thought, he has such a wonderful smile, and the light in those gray eyes is so intense, I do not understand why Mariel is not madly in love with him! Of course she is very young, she told herself stoutly, and when the duke declares himself, she will soon come to see what love can be. She shook her head and went out to find her aunt.

It rained for the following three days, straining the tempers of everyone at the inn. Mrs. Holland was not used to cooking for the quality. As she said, she was a good plain cook and she was not about to attempt any of them fancy French sauces! Consequently her meals were not anything out of the ordinary. The duke ignored them until he sat down the third evening to yet another bowl of stew.

"I see I shall have to ask the doctor more particularly when he calls tomorrow how long Greeton must remain here!" he remarked to the company raising his quizzing glass and staring at the stew. "I wonder what this meat can be?" he inquired of the bowl. "Or perhaps it is better not to ask?"

Mariel giggled as she stirred her portion. "I believe we had it last night, Your Grace. I think it is lamb!"

"Lamb!" Lady Carleton snorted in disbelief. "It is mutton, and very old, tough mutton too! And what are all these vegetables? Dear me!"

"I think it will be better for all of us when we can remove to Chatham Park," the duke continued, helping himself to bread and cheese. "I am sure the doctor will give his permission when I tell him he will soon have us all for patients as well as young Greeton if we have to continue to eat this... this..."

His voice trailed off, for he was unable to think of the correct word.

"Bowl of pottage?" Algy supplied brightly. "It is very kind of you, Your Grace, but we should not impose on your hospitality!"

Lady Carleton frowned at her son, but he did not notice.

"Perhaps Mariel and I should also return," Lady Winship said hesitantly. The duke raised his hand.

"On no account, Lady Winship! What, return where everyone can see Mariel in her condition? There are bound to be awkward questions even if Barton and Sir Percival have kept silent. It does not bear thinking of!"

"Indeed, the bruises are fading every day!" Mariel put in indignantly.

"But they are in no way gone!" the duke said imperturbably. "It will be so much better for you to remain in the country *quietly* until all traces of your adventure have disappeared, and the gossip has had a chance to die down! Besides, you can help amuse young Greeton through his convalescence. Do reconsider, Mr. Carleton! Your attendance on your friend would be most welcome, and I promise you neither of us will have to nurse him anymore, and that must be a powerful incentive!"

Algy finally agreed he would be glad to join the party if the duke was sure he would not be in the way, delighted at the thought of being in such close proximity to dear Ellen! Lady Carleton snorted.

"In the way? At Chatham Park? It is such a huge pile, an army wouldn't be in the way, am I not right, Chatham?"

The duke agreed his ancestral home was on the large side and told an amusing story of once having to send out a search party of servants to locate a guest who had wandered off to inspect the house on his own.

As it turned out, Mariel was not much help nursing John. She tried to avoid going to his room without another member of the party with her, for she had not forgotten what he had said about marriage during the curricle race, nor the look in his hazel eyes when she had first gone to sit with him. It made her very uneasy, and because she could not get outside, she was restless.

She paced up and down the parlor one afternoon, continually twitching at the curtains and complaining of the weather until Algy lost his temper.

"Oh cut line, and sit down!" he exploded. "What a fidget you are! To think it was all your fault that we are so badly placed here! But you forget that, don't you, you irresponsible chit!"

This was too much, and Mariel proceeded to tell him exactly what she had always thought of him, and it was not long before both voices were raised in anger. The duke, coming in behind Lady Winship, spoke in a cold, commanding voice.

"Stop this bickering at once, both of you!"

Algy subsided, annoyed that Ellen had seen him behaving so childishly, and Mariel tossed her head, but held her tongue.

"You are behaving like spoiled children!" the duke continued sharply. "Let us have a little more reserve and consideration for others, if you please!"

But privately, he told Lady Winship he would be glad when they could leave the inn, for being in such close proximity seemed to acerbate the tensions between Mariel and her cousin.

At last the sun shone and the doctor grudgingly agreed that John might travel the miles to Chatham Park the following day if the carriage went slowly and there were frequent stops to rest his patient. The next morning, the village of Merley had another treat as the caravan left the inn.

First there was the duke's carriage with Lady Carleton and John, propped up on many pillows and covered with shawls and blankets. He would have protested more at this invalid treatment except the trip down the narrow stairs had tired him, and his shoulder was aching again. Several of the village children were sure he must be the Prince Regent to travel in such state and curtseyed to him, for behind the large carriage came the Carletons' light one containing Lady Winship, her daughter, and their maid, and this was followed by the duke's racing curricle drawn by his chestnuts. Algy accompanied the duke with the groom up behind. The Hollands waved good-bye mournfully, sorry to lose such well-paying guests, all of whom made a mental note never to stop in Merley again, no matter how pressing the reason!

The way was long and tedious, but no one minded. On the frequent stops, everyone but John got down and stretched their legs, and at noontime, the groom produced two large hampers which had been sent with the carriage from Chatham Park, and the company had a picnic by the side of the road, the door of the coach open so John could join in the festivities.

"But how wonderful!" Mariel exclaimed, eyeing the chicken and the little biscuits filled with ham, as well as the baskets of wild strawberries and the assorted pastries and little cakes. "Oh, how glad I am that we are going to Chatham Park!"

The duke laughed at her from where he was pouring a glass of champagne for Lady Winship.

"If you are sure you will not miss that wonderful stew from the Lamb and Lion! Come to think of it, maybe it was lion after all, instead of mutton! It certainly had a singular taste!"

Everyone laughed at the duke's pleasantry, even John, who was perfectly content to sit quietly and watch his Mariel, her red hair turned to gold in the sunlight as she smiled up at him and asked him how he did.

"I am very well, thank you!" he said, waving a chicken leg gaily. Mariel and Algy wandered off down the lane to pick a bouquet of wild flowers for him while the others completed their meal. Everyone agreed that such a nursery pace was a delightful way to travel, and when the gates of Chatham Park were reached it was almost with regret.

Mariel's eyes widened when she saw the style and size of the duke's principal seat. They had traveled a long way from the road through a park of ancient trees, and when they again came to the open and she saw the acres of lawns stretching ahead of them, and the stream and gardens, as well as the four-story mansion of gray stone, endlessly extended with large wings and terraces, she was amazed. She pointed out some peacocks to her mother as their carriage swept up to the front, and Lady Winship agreed she had never seen anything quite as magnificent! Even Braxton Hall was as nothing next to such grandeur, and for a moment as she alighted from the carriage and stared up at the mansion, she felt a pang of doubt that Mariel could ever manage to be a competent chatelaine here.

They were soon escorted to comfortable bedchambers to rest before dinner. Lady Winship was pleased to find that Mariel had been placed next door, although the duke had given her the more magnificent suite of rooms. There was a charming sitting room with a balcony, a large bedroom, and the most beautiful dressing room she had ever seen, complete with bath and mirrored walls which opened to disclose large closets. On every table were vases full of creamy yellow roses, their delicate scent perfuming the rooms.

"Isn't this all the crack, Mama?" Mariel asked as she ran in to see her mother's accomodations. "Why, your rooms are even more beautiful than mine!" She inspected the combs and bottles and hand mirror on the dressing table as she spoke and added in an awed voice, "Can these be real gold and jewels?"

Lady Winship looked at the fittings and said in a small voice that she believed they were.

"Well!" Mariel exclaimed. "The duke must be as rich as Golden Ball!"

"Mariel!" her mother admonished her. "Do not speak so; it is not at all the thing. And if the duke has honored me by giving me the best rooms, it is just his kindness and politeness because I am your mother! Too good!"

Mariel opened her mouth, but then closed it thoughtfully as Annie bustled in with her mother's gown for dinner.

When Lady Carleton had learned they were all to go to Chatham Park, she had immediately sent a message to her husband in London. Telling him that both John and Mariel were recovering well, she asked him to send her dresser, Wiggans, to Chatham Park, along with a more varied and formal selection of clothes for all three ladies, for it was most important—heavily underscored—that dear Ellen look her best there, for there were sure to be formal dinners, and perhaps even dancing parties. One in particular, she added, she quite longed to attend, and had every expectation of doing so in the very near future! She signed the note with her love and then added a postscript.

> Do cancel the order for the house in Brighton, my dear, for I am sure there is no need to go there unless you are especially desirous of doing so for I am sure we can return to Oak Grove shortly!

Lord Carleton could make no sense of these heavy but obscure hints but, knowing his Daphne, followed her orders without question. He certainly had no desire for Brighton and was not even aware that Lady Carleton had planned a sojourn there since she had quite forgotten to mention it.

Lady Winship was once again attired in her sea-green silk, glad that her aunt had been so thoughtful. When Mariel was ready, they strolled together down the winding stair. Lady Winship was glad that her daughter looked better; in fact the bruises on her face were almost gone, and a light dusting of powder helped in the disguise. A footman in the duke's livery bowed and led them to the drawing room, just as the first gong for dinner sounded. The duke was lounging before the fire which took the evening chill from the large room. Mariel looked around frankly, as he came to greet them with a smile.

"What a magnificent house, Your Grace!" Lady Winship said to him. "Our rooms are lovely!"

"Have you everything you require, m'lady? You have only to ask!" the duke replied, and Lady Winship looked up at him and felt again a warm, melting feeling. He was smiling down at her, his eyes intent, and if a log had not shifted at just that moment and distracted them both, she was sure she would have blushed scarlet at her thoughts. Behind them, Mariel wandered around inspecting the duke's drawing room.

They were soon joined by Lady Carleton and her son, who came in together. Lady Carleton was able to report that John had taken no hurt from the journey and was even now fast asleep in bed, after a delightful tray supper served by the two servants the duke had so kindly provided for his care.

When the butler announced dinner, the duke escorted Lady Carleton to the dining room, Algy eagerly offering his arm to Lady Winship and saying to Mariel, "Too bad, but your mother takes precedence, you know!"

"Pooh!" Mariel retorted. "I shall try to get along unattended, and just as long as I keep you in sight, I shall not lose my way!"

Everyone laughed at her, but when they were finally

in the dining room she exclaimed, "My word! You could feed a hundred people in here! What state!"

Both the older ladies frowned at her as the duke agreed it was perhaps too massive a chamber for only five people. As they took their seats and a footman came to stand behind every chair, he added, "I was thinking that perhaps it might be pleasant to have a party or two while you are here, to liven things up! I shall see to it, for I do not want you to be bored!"

Lady Carleton beamed at him for she loved parties and told him that would be most pleasant, and then she sighed over her soup. When the duke looked at her inquiringly, she said in a contented voice, "So...so very delicious!"

"So...so very unlike the inn at Merley!" agreed Lady Winship.

It was a pleasant dinner, for after the last few days they all felt like old friends. The duke proposed a ride for Algy and Mariel in the morning and said he would be delighted to have them exercise some of his mounts; in fact he had a perfect horse for Lady Mariel, and here at Chatham she could gallop to her heart's content! Mariel smiled at him warmly for his kindness.

After the last remove, the ladies left the duke and Algy to their port and adjourned to the drawing room. Mariel went at once to the grand piano and played a few notes. Her mother urged her to sit down and play for them. Here was something that Mariel did very well, and it was an activity the duke had not had the pleasure of observing her perform. Mariel obediently searched through some music on top of the piano and was delighted to find a sonata she had learned at Lochcrae.

The other two ladies sat down before the fire, each happy in her own way to be here in such comfort, and listened contentedly as Mariel began to play. When the gentlemen joined them, she was just finishing, and at once the duke begged her to continue and to sing for them as well. He had a footman open the instrument and asked Algy to turn the pages for her.

"I will try very hard not to disgrace my teacher!" she said with a special smile for her mother. "But it has been some time since I practiced!" She had no need to worry, for she performed very well, and Algy, although not a music lover, was surprised at her skill.

The duke joined the ladies by the fire, although Lady Winship wished he would attend more closely to Mariel and not feel he had to entertain them, as her daughter began another sonata, but all in all, she had to be happy at the way the evening turned out.

Mariel was up early the next morning, and after a hasty breakfast, she went outside dressed in her best habit to join the duke and Algy. They all stood together enjoying the balmy sunshine while the horses were brought round from the stables. Mariel was delighted with the spirited little mare the duke had chosen for her, all black except for one white stocking, and it was not long before they were cantering away down the drive. Lady Winship smiled as she watched them from a window in her sitting room, and then she went to join her aunt for a visit to John Greeton.

He was up and seated at a breakfast table when the ladies were announced and would have risen to greet them if Lady Carleton had not insisted he remain seated.

"Should you be up, sir?" she asked anxiously. "I am sure the doctor would not approve...."

John was feeling very low, for he had heard of the riding party, and was determined to get well as soon as he could before the duke managed to fix his interest with Mariel, so he answered shortly.

"I shall do very well, ladies! I cannot stay in bed all

the time, and after all, there is nothing wrong with my legs!" He had spoken as if to his own mother, and now he recalled himself and smiled to remove the sting.

They reluctantly agreed that perhaps he was right, but begged him not to dress and come downstairs today, and he was forced to promise, although he seemed unwilling to listen to such good advice, and it was not until Lady Winship said she would send Mariel up to keep him company as soon as she returned from her ride that he smiled and finally agreed.

Lady Carleton sighed as they left his room. "MEN! And especially young men! They are so difficult when they are ill," she confided to her niece. "Algy was always this way when he was sick, Ellen! How could I ever forget the mumps or the chicken pox!"

Fortunately, for Lady Winship had no desire to hear every detail of Algy's childhood diseases, the ladies were met at the bottom of the stairs by the duke's housekeeper. This pleasant lady said that the duke had arranged for her to take them over the house after they had breakfasted, and Lady Winship was delighted, although her aunt would only agree to see the main section, for, as she said, "It must be miles from one end of the house to the other! We shall be quite worn down!"

In spite of her warning, Lady Winship found the morning very pleasant, and when their tour was over and Lady Carleton had gone to see the chef so she might copy a recipe she had especially enjoyed at dinner, she went out on the front terrace to get some air. As she was standing there admiring the handsome peacocks on the lawn, a smart perch phaeton came sweeping up the drive, followed closely by the riding party. When it had come to a halt at the front steps, the duke dismounted promptly in order to assist a small lady down from the perch. She was dressed in scarlet, with a very smart driving hat that was curled around with white ostrich plumes. It was stunning with her dark hair and eyes. She held out her hand, laughing at something the duke was saying, and when she was safely on the ground, she put her arms around him and hugged him. Lady Winship was too far away to hear what they were saying, but she could see only too closely the warm smile the duke gave to this lady before he introduced her to the others. After a few moments of conversation he was seen to urge her to come in, but she shook her head and was soon back in her seat, her groom beside her. With a final flourish of her whip, and a last tinkling laugh, she tooled away down the drive.

"I quite agree with you, Ellen!" Lady Carleton said from behind her niece, startling her considerably. "I myself have never cared for that type of small lively brunette! And she was so very forward too!"

Lady Winship tried to smile as the riding party came towards them.

"She was very beautiful, wasn't she? I wonder who she might be?"

"I am sure we will find out!" Lady Carleton sniffed in disdain.

Mariel ran ahead of the men and hugged her mother. "We had a splendid ride, Mama! And did you see Lady Galley? What a rig! If only I could drive something as smart as that!"

The duke came up behind her and saluted the ladies as Mariel added, "She has promised to come to the duke's party too! What fun that will be!"

Neither lady appeared to be overwhelmed with joy at the prospect, and Lady Winship felt a pang of disquiet which she put down to the appearance of such a dear friend of the duke who might be a threat to Mariel's chances.

She questioned the duke during luncheon about his

neighbors, and since she was careful not to arouse any suspicion of any particular interest, she learned only that Lady Galley was a widow whose late husband had been killed in Spain while serving with Wellington, and that they had all known each other forever. It did not reassure her in the slightest!

TWELVE

Preparations for the party went on, but not the tiniest stir or bustle came to the attention of the guests, and even if it had been a grand ball instead of a small dinner party and dance for a mere fifty guests, the results would have been the same. The duke's staff was extremely well trained.

Mariel continued to ride every day although the duke was often unable to accompany her, for there was a great deal of estate business that had to be attended to after his long stay in town. She visited John regularly, but always in the company of her mother or her aunt, and one day, while Lady Carleton was busy arranging some flowers she had brought to his room, she looked up to see him regarding her darkly, almost as if he knew she was afraid to be alone with him, she thought wildly. Fortunately Lady Carleton did not notice her sudden blush, but John nodded his head as if he could read her mind, which made Mariel very uneasy. She would have stopped visiting him, but that would surely be remarked on, and a perverse part of her looked forward eagerly to their meetings.

Lady Winship especially enjoyed the beautiful gardens of Chatham Park, and could be found there most afternoons, strolling the paths to admire the many blooms, feeding the swans on the lake, or sitting under a great elm tree, reading. The duke had had some lawn chairs placed there for his guests, and as soon as John was able, he preferred to spend his time there, propped up on pillows in a long chair and trying not to stare at Mariel too obviously, for he was generally joined by the other members of the house party, all of whom agreed it was a perfect way to spend a warm summer afternoon.

One day when Algy had wandered out to the elm tree, he found himself alone, except for a newspaper and a tall pitcher of iced punch and some glasses which the servants had left on a small table. He was delighted when he saw Lady Winship coming across the lawns towards him, and his heart beat faster as he watched her. He prayed that John would remain indoors, and Mariel and his mother find some other source of amusement that afternoon. Lady Winship inquired how he did with her lovely smile, and then she sat down and opened her book. The book had become a defense, for she was never really at ease with her young cousin. What there was about him she could not say, but in order not to be trapped in conversation *à deux,* she always brought her copy of Sir Walter Scott's poems with her.

For a while the two were silent, as Algy tried to find something of interest in the newspaper, but it seemed to be made up of extremely boring reports, for he soon dropped it to the grass with a sigh. Lady Winship looked up inquiringly.

"There is nothing in the papers, cousin!" Algy complained. "Lord, why the editors think anyone would be interested in an account of the cows in Green Park and their attendant milkmaids, or a revival of one of Sheridan's early plays I have no idea! Everyone of interest must have left town!"

At his peevish tone, Lady Winship raised her brows, and he added quickly, "I am sorry to be such poor company, but I find the country boring. There is so little to do! Won't you read to me for a while? I know I would enjoy that!"

Remembering that it was Mariel's fault that Algy was incarcerated in the country and also that if she read to him she would not have to converse, Lady Winship agreed and searched her book for something she felt might be to Algy's taste.

The duke, coming up from the stables heard her voice from behind the hedge and paused to listen. He had come this way expressly for the purpose of finding her, hopefully alone. Suddenly he heard Algy say, "You must be fond of Scott, Ellen, you read him so often! He is one of my favorites too!"

Lady Winship agreed she admired the poet and began to read in her soft, musical voice. The duke, annoyed that Algy was present, would have gone away then except that Lady Winship, who had unfortunately chosen to read from "Marmion," had reached the lines

"So faithful in love, so dauntless in war,
There never was knight like young Lochinvar.
For a laggard in love, and a dastard in war,
Was to wed the fair Ellen of brave Lochinvar..."

At that, all Algy's careful self-control disappeared, and he rose from his chair and knelt before her, saying passionately, "Fair Ellen indeed! *Dearest* Ellen! Allow me to lay my heart and my love at your feet, like Lochinvar of old!"

Lady Winship sat frozen, staring down with something very like horror at her handsome young cousin, his blue eyes shining with ardor, and his blond hair blowing slightly in the breeze. At this sign of seeming acquiescence, Algy took her unresisting hands in his and continued fervently, "I have loved you so long, Ellen! Say that my love is not in vain, I beg you!"

"So it was *you*," Lady Winship said faintly. *"You* who sent me all those flowers and gifts! Oh do get up, Algy! This is ridiculous!"

Algy frowned. Surely this was a singular way to reply to such a passionate avowal of love! "Ridiculous? How can you say so? I fear I have shocked you with my ardor, but indeed, dearest Ellen, I could not remain silent any longer! Give me a ray of hope! Say you will marry me!"

The duke, his mouth open in very unducal amazement, would have rounded the hedge at this point and told young Carleton to take himself off at once, when Lady Winship spoke again.

"Come, cousin, sit down again and let us talk of this calmly. I will go away immediately if you do not!"

Her voice was so controlled now, and her order so quickly obeyed, that the duke remained where he was, shamelessly listening.

"You have only to command me and I obey, my love!" Algy said as he regained his seat.

Ignoring this statement, Lady Winship said, "I had no idea of the state of your mind, cousin, for it is quite, quite impossible! You do realize that I am thirty-five, almost fifteen years older than you, do you not? I could never consider you as anything beyond a young relation. Come Algy, be sensible, you must see that it would not do!"

"Do not speak to me of age!" Algy declared in a ringing voice. "You are ageless, and your beauty will never fade! What care we for convention my love? Be bold, and dare with me!" He ruined this poetic declaration by adding peevishly, "Besides, there is only twelve years difference between us!"

The duke was hard put to remain in his hiding place at this, but Lady Winship said calmly, "I wonder if you would think so when I am sixty-two and gray and wrinkled, and you with a mere fifty in your dish, and in your prime! You only think yourself in love, my dear, and when you are happily married with your children around you, you will look back on this afternoon and wonder how you could ever have imagined yourself in love with me!"

"Never!" declared Algy vehemently. "I shall never marry if you deny me! There is no woman on earth who can compare with you!!"

For the first time that afternoon, the duke agreed with him wholeheartedly, as Lady Winship rose and said with quiet dignity, "I see there is no reasoning with you, Algy! You will attend to me now though, if you please! I do not love you, I will never love you, for to me you will always be a very young cousin, whose life I shall watch unfold with family pride. I advise you to remember this for I was never more serious in my life! Forget this infatuation and never speak of it again, for if you do, I shall be forced to bring it to your father's attention!"

Algy was stunned by this firm statement and swallowed several times. It was impossible to continue to make love to a lady who treated you like a child and threatened to tell your father on you, and so he rose with as much dignity as he could muster and said, "I shall do as you request, cousin, since you have blighted all my hopes and dreams, but I shall never forget you, never, for you shall always remain my dearest Ellen in my heart!"

On these ringing words he left her, hoping that she watched him as he strode away, his head high, but since it would have ruined his pose to turn, he could not see that Ellen had buried her face in a handkerchief. It was just as well, for he might have taken heart and thought she was regretting her impetuous behavior and been tempted to try again. The duke, coming around the hedge, was afraid that she was upset and weeping, and he hastened to her side.

"Impossible young puppy!" he exclaimed. "Dear Ellen, do not cry! How dare that young idiot upset you!"

Lady Winship lowered her handkerchief, and the duke stopped in confusion, for she was smiling and trying not to laugh.

"Oh dear, Your Grace, I beg you to forgive me, but I could not destroy him completely by laughing in his face! You must not think me unfeeling, but all those passionate avowals and rehearsed periods... it was too much!"

She composed herself and put her handkerchief away and rescued Scott who had fallen unheeded to the grass. The duke seated himself in Algy's chair as she continued.

"How very ridiculous that scene was! The worst melodrama ever written could not compare to it! I must tell you that I have been assaulted daily with the most silly love notes and letters, all unsigned, as well as flowers and gifts, with never a clue to the identity of my mysterious suitor until today! And then to find out it was Algy—ALGY!! So *that* was why Dortle could not place the man...."

The duke, who had been watching her carefully, nodded his head although he had no idea who "Dortle" might be.

"I will not apologize for eavesdropping, m'lady, for I was prepared to come to your rescue if you should need me. My compliments on your handling of the situation! You not only firmly repulsed him, you left him with his dignity as well, something not all women would have done with such tact and kindness!"

Lady Winship blushed at these words, her heart beating a little faster, but she only said carelessly, "There was no need to cut him up, but I give you my word, I have never encouraged his feelings! There is so much disparity in our ages, and I have been a widow so many years—why, my daughter is not much younger than Algy himself! It is Mariel's marriage that I think of now, most certainly not my own, for I do not intend to marry again!"

At these daring words, spoken so bravely by Lady Winship, the duke rose and began to pace up and down, pausing only to break off a particularly beautiful rose, which he brought back to her. She took it hesitantly and, when she looked up to thank him, was astounded by the warm, intent look on his face. It confused her, and she buried her face in the rose as the duke spoke, his voice suddenly harsh.

"Now it is you who are being ridiculous, my dear! You not marry again? What a waste! Of course you must marry! Forgive me for saying so, but I do not consider your daughter in any way ready for that blessed state—give her a few more years and then we shall see, but for now, do not consider it! At seventeen she is a mere baby, with about as much sense as one too! What she needs is a father, not a husband!"

He stopped, afraid he had gone too far. Besides, it was not his intention to let her think he was only proposing to her because her daughter needed male parental guidance. Lady Winship looked up at him, her face white with shock. Before he could speak again, she put out a hand blindly to deter him and rose, her skirts swirling as she turned away.

"You must excuse me, Your Grace!" she said formally. "I find I do not feel well this afternoon, and the scene with Algy has upset me more than I thought!"

She hurried away across the lawns, forgetting her book and dropping the rose heedlessly as she ran.

The duke stood and watched her until she gained the terrace steps, and then he bent and picked up the poems and the rose he had given her, a small rueful smile on his face. He sat down with them in his hands, staying beneath the elm for some time, alone with his thoughts.

Ellen in the meantime had hurried upstairs, praying she would not meet anyone until she had had a chance to compose herself. Had she been misinterpreting all the duke's attentions to her daughter, she wondered? And if he had no intention of proposing to Mariel, why had he invited them here? Perhaps she had not heard him correctly? That must be it, for the duke had been so constant in his regard, so quick to assist Mariel whenever she was in difficulty, so often at the Winships' sides! What could he have meant, a father, not a husband? Oh no, she was imagining things, perhaps because if she told herself the truth, she had to admit her own attraction for him. But cut Mariel out? Mariel who *must* be in love with the duke, who showed by her easy manners and ready smile for him how much she cared! It was impossible that it could be otherwise! Besides, she really *did* not contemplate marriage again ... did she?

All these questions whirled in her mind as she paced up and down her sitting room, trying to think, until she was tired and went to lie down on her bed. She was soon fast asleep, and so she missed the dressing bell. When Annie came in to see why she had not been summoned, she woke with a start. It all came flooding back, and she put her hands to her head in distraction.

"Oh Annie, I cannot go down to dinner tonight; I have such a headache! Please have Mariel excuse me to the others! I am sure I will feel more the thing in the morning if I remain quietly here and I am not disturbed by anyone."

Annie helped her to undress, and then she drew the curtains, promising to relay the message, and Lady Winship was left alone. She was startled by a knock on her door a little while later, but it was only the housekeeper, Mrs. Brumstead, with a tray of supper. As Lady Winship sat up in bed, the housekeeper arranged her pillows behind her, and then curtseyed and begged her not to hesitate to ring if there were anything she required. As she left the room and softly closed the door behind her, Lady Winship stared down at the delicious food and realized she was hungry. Hungry, that is, until she saw the book of poems on the tray with a yellow rose on top. She picked up the book and a note fell out which she opened with trembling fingers.

"I hope you will feel better in the morning, Lady Winship," the duke began formally. "Please allow me to return these things which you dropped in the garden, and to wish you a very good night. Ainsworth."

There was nothing there to make her blush, but she did, and after she had eaten as much as she wanted, she put the rose in a vase on her night table where she could see it before she went to sleep.

The next few days remaining before the party passed in some confusion. Lady Carleton was worried about Algy, who seemed so sunk in deep depression she was sure something must be dreadfully wrong. She mentioned it over and over to Ellen, who thought she would scream if she had to discuss Algy's moods one more time. Of course she could have excused herself, but since she never left Lady Carleton's side, this was quite impossible. The duke smiled grimly when he saw her so constantly with her unsuspecting *duenna*. The chairs under the elm remained vacant, and there was no way for him to see her alone. Truly he hesitated to do so, for he felt he had been much too plain in stating his intentions and did not want to upset her again until he had discovered a way to tell her what was in his heart.

Mariel, as well as John, attempted to cheer Algy up from what he privately considered an interesting gloom, and he sincerely hoped that his pallor would wring the lady's heart to the point she would reconsider his offer. He sent her intense brooding looks whenever he dared, until the duke told him in no uncertain terms one evening as they were leaving the dining room to rejoin the ladies after their port to cut line and stop annoying Lady Winship.

"You must know, Carleton," the duke said grimly, "it is very bad ton to continue to badger a lady after she has refused you!"

Unaware up to this time that his passionate declaration had been overheard, and by that arbiter of fashion, the Duke of Chatham himself, Algy blushed and excused himself. He began to feel he had made a fool of himself, and this did nothing to restore his spirits.

Of all the group only Lady Carleton and the duke were still at ease, and the duke, for his part, was so pleasant, teasing Mariel in quite the old way, that Lady Winship was almost sure there had been no basis for her imaginings, and that all would still be well.

The evening of the ball arrived, and Lady Winship

spent a great deal of time in Mariel's room, helping Annie dress her daughter in a new gown that had just been delivered from town. It was a soft beige muslin, banded in deep-copper ribbons, and she had matching sandals of the same copper shade. Lady Winship had asked the gardener for a few roses, and these she fastened at her daughter's corsage and placed artfully in her hair. Finally she stood back, as Mariel sighed in relief, and said she had never seen her daughter looking so well!

Mariel twirled around, admiring her image in the glass, and then she said, "I wish you had a new gown too, Mama! And you have spent so much time on me, you will have to rush to be ready yourself! Let me help you!"

But this she was not allowed to do, Annie saying she would only get in the way, and her mother declaring there was very little to do since she planned to wear her green silk and the Carleton emeralds, generously donated yet again by her aunt. But even though she did not linger over her toilette, the Winships were the last guests down, the carriages even then beginning to come up the drive. Lady Carleton noted with satisfaction that the duke, although courteously attending to her, kept glancing anxiously at the staircase and, when the Winships finally appeared, had a smile of relief and satisfaction on his handsome face as he hurried forward to greet them, his gray eyes warm with approval. Lady Winship of course smiled as he bowed over her hand, but as soon as the butler announced the first arrivals, hurried away to join her aunt. Mariel stood chatting with Algy and John, who was making his first public appearance since the accident. He could not dance since he still wore a sling, but he was determined to be present and keep an eye on Mariel and the duke. He dared to whisper to her, when Algy turned aside for a moment, that she looked very beautiful this evening, and he was sorry he could not ask for a dance. The admiring look in his hazel eyes made her blush, and she lightly changed the subject, wondering why her heart was behaving in such a jumpy fashion!

Algy promised to keep John company so he would not be bored, but whether he would get to keep his promise was doubtful, for once again he was attired in his smart London evening dress, and he drew the eyes of several young ladies from the neighborhood who appeared much in awe of such a handsome young beau. They were obviously waiting eagerly to be presented to such a paragon as soon as they could manage it, and this interest did much to restore a sense of self-esteem, so badly shattered by Lady Winship's denial.

This lady, conversing with some of the early arrivals, had her back turned to the entrance and was startled when she heard the duke say, close behind her, "Allow me to present a very dear old friend, Lady Winship!" As she turned, she was hard put to keep a smile on her face, for there was Lady Galley standing as close as she could manage it to the duke! Tiny she might be, but she was as formidable an opponent as any goddess! Not only was she beautiful with her dark hair and eyes and perfect complexion, she also had classical features and a tempting rosy mouth. Both ladies smiled at each other, although Lady Winship was sick to see the lady clinging so possessively to the duke's arm and was hard put to greet her calmly. It seemed to her that the duke looked down at the lady so fondly, it was almost as if he had already claimed her for his own! She was again dressed in red—this time a crimson velvet cut extremely low over her voluptuous breasts. A rope of pearls ending in a large ruby pendant called attention to her décolletage, and Ellen felt something very like hate rising in her own breast. The lady came only to the duke's shoulder, but she clung so closely to his arm they appeared to be the most intimate of friends, and the evening was from that point ruined for Lady Winship. What chance would Mariel have against such a polished mature beauty, she thought sadly, her eyes going to her daughter's slight, young figure.

She was glad to be separated from the lady at table by a few places, and although she conversed with General Adams on her left and a Mr. Rannerly on her right with every indication of pleasure, she did not miss the way Lady Galley often bent towards the duke from where she was seated at his left hand, and how he put his head back and laughed heartily at something she said. Mariel had been placed further away, between John Greeton and a young man of the neighborhood who appeared quite taken with her, and she never glanced at the duke or appeared to realize that unless she were very careful all her chances would be quite cut up! Lady Winship barely tasted the delicious food or sipped the several excellent wines that were presented with each course, and it was with a sense of vast relief that she rose and left the table with the other ladies.

Lady Carleton came to sit beside her in the ballroom and said tartly, "I am sure velvet is a most unfortunate choice for such a warm evening, Ellen! Your gown is so much more attractive, and you are looking especially beautiful!"

Lady Winship looked up startled. "What has that to say to anything, aunt?" And then feeling she had been too abrupt, she added, "Of course I am glad you think so! And do you not feel Mariel is in her best looks, too? She is so young, so fresh, perhaps... at least I hope so... the duke will propose to her tonight!"

Lady Carleton snorted as the gentlemen appeared.

"I never thought you were a fool, Ellen, but you are far from the mark there!"

Before she could continue, the musicians began to play and the duke opened the ball with Lady Galley. Ellen was glad to see he asked Mariel to dance next. She herself was engaged with Mr. Rannerly for the first dance and General Adams for the second. When it ended, she saw the duke approach the musicians and then come towards her quickly to ask her to dance. She nodded as the musicians struck up a waltz and soon found herself held tightly in the duke's arms as he smiled down at her.

"I am so glad you wore that gown, Lady Winship," he said easily. "It is one of my favorites for I remember you were wearing it the first evening we met; it matches your eyes so beautifully!"

His voice was warm and intimate, and when Ellen tried to draw away from those strong arms, she found she was unable to do so. This angered her a little, so she replied, "Oh yes, that was the night that Mariel wore yellow as I recall, and you were so kind as to dance with her, even though she had just disgraced herself by galloping in the park!"

The duke had no reply to this artless statement, and Ellen glanced up to see a tiny frown on his face. When he saw she was looking at him, he smiled and changed the subject.

He danced once more with Mariel and yet again with Lady Winship, who was glad it was a country dance so they were often separated in the set. She did not like the breathless way she felt when they waltzed together and he put his arm so closely around her. She was glad Mariel was so popular, but she wished her daughter did not treat the duke so casually, almost as casually as she did her cousin! If only she had pointed out the value of a melting glance or intimate smile somewhere in Mariel's training! And why did young Mr. Greeton frown so whenever the duke was dancing with Mariel or when she was surrounded by other young men?

She was surprised to see her aunt Daphne in serious conversation with Lady Galley at one point during the evening, but she missed the satisfied smile on that lady's face when Lady Galley left her to dance. It seemed a very long evening, and she began to feel the beginnings of a headache by the time the guests began to take their leave. The duke did not seek Mariel out again, and Lady Winship went up to bed with despair in her heart. She was so preoccupied she did not see the loving smile the duke sent her as she prepared to mount the stairs, but Mariel did not miss it, and her mouth formed a small "oh" of astonishment.

Of all the house party, only Mariel and Lady Carleton slept easily that night. Algy tossed and turned as he wished he could leave Chatham Park as soon as ever might be; the duke was kept awake by wondering what he was to do next; John was angry with the duke's continued attentions to Mariel; and Lady Winship was in despair, so sure the duke was enamored with Lady Galley!

THIRTEEN

The following morning the duke was not surprised to find he had the breakfast table to himself, for although he had to rise early to be about the estate, he fully expected his guests to sleep late after the evening's festivities. He was just finishing a hearty breakfast, and had poured himself another cup of coffee, when John Greeton appeared. The duke greeted him cordially and asked after his injuries and was surprised when the young man answered him so shortly. After John had helped himself to some of the dishes on the sideboard, he took a seat near the duke and stared at his plate.

The duke raised one eyebrow and said, "Not hungry, John?"

John flushed a little and then seemed to come to a

decision for he pushed his plate away and turned to the duke with an air of great purpose.

"Your Grace!" he began, and then had to clear his throat before he could continue. "I know I have no right to ask, but I *must* know! What are your intentions towards Mariel, if you please?"

Nonplussed, the duke returned his stare. "My intentions? Towards Mariel?"

"Yes, that is what I asked!" Greeton said, clenching his teeth. "You have been so very particular in your attentions to the lady for such a long time, and I would like to know to what purpose! If you are thinking of marrying her, let me tell you that you are much too old for her! It would be a crime to marry such a young girl to a man of your years!" He stopped, afraid he had gone too far and had offended the duke, but when he looked at him he was stunned to see that far from being angry, the duke was having trouble controlling a smile.

"As it happens, I agree with you, John!" he said easily. "But it was not very kind of you to point out my advanced age as a serious detriment! I am not exactly drooling and senile, you know!"

"I beg your pardon, I'm sure, Your Grace," John said formally, and then added, for he was not at all to be swayed from his question, "But why then do you shower the Winships with such distinguished attentions, and why did you invite them to Chatham Park?"

Now it was the duke's turn to flush, his smile quite gone.

"There is really no reason why I should answer your questions, John," he said finally. "Let me tell you however that I never had any intention of marrying Mariel; I desire a very different lady!" He stopped abruptly and put down his coffee cup with a snap.

"I do not understand!" John muttered. "Where Mariel is . . . you are always there too! I was sure you were about to ask for her hand, and I decided I must try and stop you! To try and make Mariel Duchess of Chatham would be folly and would make her miserable! Besides, I . . . well . . ."

"You need not fear for Mariel; she would refuse me if I did offer for her!" the duke said as John faltered. "But as it happens, I am in complete agreement. She *is* much too young for me, as I have pointed out to her mother!" He stopped again, and John looked at him sharply.

"Does Lady Winship wish you to marry Mariel?" he asked.

"Of course she does! Oh, I do not accuse her of being mercenary, or wanting a great state marriage for her daughter, but she is of the opinion that Mariel loves me—lord, what a tangle!"

The duke shook his head as John exclaimed, "So Mariel is *not* in love with you! I was almost sure she didn't know her own heart yet and I am surprised that Lady Winship doesn't understand. But why do you not tell her so if that is the case?"

The duke threw out his hands in defeat. "I see I must be honest with you, John, but what I tell you must remain only in this room, do you understand?"

He looked so fierce that John could only nod his head.

"Well then," the duke continued, somewhat reluctantly, "I don't want to be Mariel's husband, I want to be her stepfather! I did not realize that Lady Winship would take my attentions as a sign of affection for her daughter, and by the time I discovered it, it was too late to change things! In order to be near her—I was forced to escort her daughter—what a farce!"

He rose to pace the breakfast room while John stared at him in shock.

"What I am to do about this imbroglio I do not know! Have you any suggestions, young John?"

John was speechless, so the duke continued. "And what is *your* interest in this, by the way? Are you in love with Mariel yourself?"

John blushed bright red, but he said manfully, "As to that, yes, I am! When I first saw Mariel she reminded me of marigolds, with her copper hair and pert ways, but I have been afraid to press her, thinking her attracted to you! But after what you have told me, I shall not hesitate any longer!" He paused, and then said more formally, "I have just inherited my great-uncle Malcolm's estate in Scotland. It is very near Lochcrae—Mariel knows it—and I meant to remove there as soon as the Winships returned home. Now however, I can tell Mariel of my love and take her back to Scotland with me as my bride!"

The duke applauded this excellent reasoning and wished him every success as John beamed happily. He said, almost as an afterthought, that he wished he could see a way to help the duke out of his predicament, but nothing helpful came to his mind.

"Yes, it is a problem!" the duke agreed. "But you think only of your marigold, and remember, not a word to anyone!"

He left the room abruptly and John began to eat his breakfast with great appetite. What a wonderful day it had turned out to be after all!

As the duke reached the hall, his butler came forward and presented him with a note on a silver salver. The duke read it frowning. It was from Lady Carleton and it begged the indulgence of a few moments of his time. The butler said that the lady was even then in the red salon, and the duke took a deep breath and prepared to join her, putting off his business once again.

As he bowed over her hand, the lady said, "So good

of you, Your Grace! I have a problem, and I wish your advice in solving it!"

"I am at your service, m'lady," the duke said, leading her to a chair, and steeling himself for whatever difficulty had now occurred.

Lady Carleton seemed to have trouble beginning. "This is so awkward—oh dear, but I am *sure* I was not mistaken!—But what if I were wrong? How embarrassing! Of course it would give you a disgust of me, but how am I to find out if I do not ask you?"

"How indeed?" the duke asked, his eyes twinkling now. "But you will never know until you *do* ask me, you know, for I have not the slightest idea what you are talking about!"

"Oh, you must not mind me. Carleton says he cannot follow my conversation to this day, and we have been married forever, you know! But not to put too fine a point on it, I see I shall have to finish this bout with the gloves off, as Algy would say...."

The duke tried hard not to picture Lady Carleton in the ring in order to control his expression as she took a deep breath.

"Very well!" she said with great resolution. "What are your intentions if you please, Your Grace, towards my niece, Lady Winship?"

She seemed flustered, but still she stared at him defiantly.

"Are you quite sure you do not wish to know my intentions towards Mariel, Lady Carleton?" the duke inquired in an interested way.

"Mariel? Of course not! I know you have no *tendre* for her at all!"

"What a relief, m'lady! I have already been taxed with that question this morning from young Greeton! He seemed to feel I was about to propose to Mariel, and he told me in no uncertain terms that I was much too old for her!" Lady Carleton would have spoken, but he put up his hand. "Of course you are more astute, and you are right! I love Lady Winship, but since she is expecting me to marry her daughter, I have not found a way to broach the subject!"

He moved abruptly to the fireplace and lounged against the mantel, looking broodingly into the fire. "Little did I suspect when I arose this morning that I was going to have to discuss such personal matters with the entire household before lunch!"

"Now Ainsworth!" Lady Carleton said soothingly. "I am sure there will be no need to discuss it with another soul except, of course, with Ellen. And if I may offer a word of advice, why do you not do just that? Faint heart never won fair lady, you know!"

The duke groaned. "I tried, the other day in the garden, by telling her that Mariel needed a father more than she needed a husband, and Ellen reacted by running away from me! Since that time she has never left your side! I am afraid I frightened her...."

"Pish! Frightened indeed! She is no young girl in her first season, and if she ran away it is because you have given her every reason to hope that Mariel was to be your duchess! I think you must be honest with her, and if you do it as well as I suspect you can, she will soon admit she loves you herself!"

"Has she said so?" the duke asked eagerly.

Lady Carleton shook her head. "No, of course not, she still maintains that you are in love with Mariel! But I suspect she is, and I have heard...I mean, a man of your experience...well! I am sure you will know just what to say...or perhaps, more importantly, *do!* Oh dear, it is not my place I am sure to be teaching you how to make love!" She began to search in her reticule for her handkerchief, in some confusion, as the duke began to chuckle.

"Let me reassure you, m'lady, that I have some small experience with members of your sex!"

Lady Carleton sniffed. "So I have always understood! But the problem, Ainsworth, is that Algy is most anxious to return to town, and if we go, the Winships of course must go with us! That is why I made so bold as to ask you because I do not think I can restrain him much longer! I do not know what it is, but he has not been happy here in spite of your wonderful hospitality. So you see, it would be a great help if you could talk to Ellen as quickly as possible—perhaps today?" She leaned forward on the edge of her seat and smiled at him expectantly.

The duke stared down at her. "Of course you are right! There is no reason why not; I will see what I can do! Restrain your son until tomorrow, Lady Carleton, if you please!"

Daphne said she was sure she could manage one more day, and they parted amiably, the duke finally escaping the house and striding briskly towards the stables.

But alas, he was not to reach them undetected. As he crossed the lawn, he heard someone calling, and turned impatiently to see Mariel running towards him.

"Thank you for waiting, Your Grace!" she said, panting a little as she came up. "I have something of particular importance to speak to you about!"

The duke threw up his hands. "Of course you do! Why should you be any different from the rest?" Mariel looked confused, so he took her arm and walked with her slowly back towards the gardens.

"And what is this important matter?" he inquired.

"I want to know why you do not ask my mother to marry you!" Mariel said bluntly, in quite the most straightforward declaration of the morning.

"Mariel," the duke said firmly, "you don't think that

perhaps this is just a little—a mere trifle to be sure—indelicate of you to ask?"

Mariel tossed her head. "Of course not, for you know I was never missish! I have seen the way you look at her; there is no mistaking your feelings! Why, when we went upstairs to bed last night, I was positive from your expression as you said good-night that you loved her. And since you *do*," she continued firmly, "whatever is the matter with you that you do not tell her so?"

The duke stopped short and put a hand to his head. "Lord, what else this morning? It only needs Algy asking my advice on winning his ladylove to complete the scene! The reason, my dear perceptive Mariel, is that your mother wants me to offer for you and has been expecting me to ask for her permission to do so for many weeks!"

"Marry *ME?*" she asked in complete disbelief. "You cannot be serious! Why, you are so *old!*"

"Thank you!" the duke said dryly. "Any conceits that I have ever harbored have been vanquished most thoroughly this morning!"

"I am sure I did not mean to offend you, Your Grace," Mariel said quickly, slightly flustered now. "But after all, you are about the age my father was when mama married him, and she promised me I should never be forced into such a match!"

"I rather suspect she thinks you are in love with me," the duke said, idly inspecting a rosebush, and manfully keeping his composure.

"In love? With *YOU?*"

"I wish you would not act as if it were the most repugnant thing you had ever heard, Mariel!" the duke snapped. "I could tell you the names of many ladies who have fancied themselves in love with me over the years! It is not an impossibility you know, even if you seem to find it so!"

Mariel took his arm and smiled up at him. "Now, now! I apologize for hurting your feelings," she said soothingly, "but I could never fall in love with you! How silly of mama! Why, history would repeat itself, for she was not at all happy with my father...."

The duke knew he should not ask questions, but he could not restrain himself. "Was she truly forced to marry Lord Winship? I had no idea! I hope it did not give her a dislike of marriage!"

Mariel hastened to reassure him. "Well, she said he was everything that was kind, but he seems to have been a cold man who had no interest in parties, or gaiety, or ... or anything a young girl might like! And she assured me that when the time came I should choose my own husband, and as long as he was respectable, she would not stand in my way!"

"How fortunate!" the duke said. "Now we only have to find a respectable man who is at the same time willing to marry you! Do you know, Mariel, in spite of that seeming to be an insurmountable problem, I do believe there may be a candidate waiting in the wings—do you agree?"

Mariel blushed and shook her head and then decided to ignore this raillery. "I have no interest in marriage, as I have tried to tell mama from the beginning! Why, it was only for her sake that I consented to come to London for the season. My Uncle James said I was being selfish to refuse, but really, all I ever wanted to do was stay at Lochcrae and help manage the estate!"

"I, for one, am glad you did not, Mariel, for if you had, I might never have met your mother!"

"So you *do* love her! Wonderful! And even if I do not want you as a husband, I shall not mind having you as a father, you know!" Mariel said generously. "But how are we to convince mama that she should marry you?" She thought for a moment and then said, "I know! I will go to her and explain everything...."

"You will do no such thing!" the duke said, stopping short and grasping her hard by the arms. "You will keep right out of it, Mariel, do you understand?" He shook her a little, and her eyes widened.

"Well! Of course if you feel that way, but I was only trying to help!"

"I can do without your help, or your aunt's or young Greeton's either! Thank heavens there is no danger of Algy offering his services as well!" the duke exclaimed thankfully in the tones of a man most pressed. "Now attend me well, Mariel, for if I find you have meddled, I shall be very, very angry!"

Mariel stared up at his steely gray eyes and nodded. "Perhaps I shall be sorry to have you for a father after all," she said in a small voice.

"Nonsense! We shall deal splendidly together!" the duke assured her, releasing her arms. "And you will like to have the chestnuts to drive, and your own perch phaeton like Lady Galley's; that is if you condescend to leave Scotland and visit us once in a while!"

Mariel thanked him for his invitation and told him in a very dignified way that he was being silly to think she would need to be bribed by a team and phaeton, and that she especially looked forward to coming to Chatham Park in the winter when even she had to admit Scotland was a bit dreary!

They parted in great accord after the duke warned her once again to keep her tongue between her teeth, which Mariel promised to do, and then he went at once to the stables. He had been so delayed that it was unlikely there was much he could accomplish for the rest of the morning, but he felt the need to put a little space between himself and the Hall for awhile. When he should have been inspecting the new drainage ditch, however, he found himself rehearsing the speech he planned to make to Ellen, and as he discussed fertilizer and the haying with one of his farmers, found himself in a rush to return, for he had no confidence that Mariel would not blurt something out to her mother before he could plead his case.

He hurried back to the Hall and changed his riding clothes before he went in search of her. She was not in the breakfast room, nor strolling up and down the terrace, and the chairs under the elm were empty. He stood by the window for a moment, deeply frustrated, and wished for the first time that Chatham Park were not so huge. She might be anywhere! Finally he asked his butler if he had seen Lady Winship and was told that the lady had gone into the library some little while ago. The duke took a deep breath and went to find her, after telling the butler that he was not to be disturbed for any reason, which caused that good man to stare at his retreating back with a great deal of interest.

There was a small fire burning in the library, and the duke was glad to see Ellen curled up on a window seat with a book in her hand, quite alone. She had been so sure she would not be disturbed here that she was startled as the door closed and she looked up and saw the duke smiling at her as he crossed the room to her side. She rose, smoothing down her simple aqua morning gown, and curtseyed to him, her heart beating fast. For a long moment he looked down at her, and she returned his gaze wonderingly, her green eyes wide, and delicate color coming to her cheeks.

"My dear Lady Winship," he began formally, in a somewhat strained voice, "no, that's not right! My dear Ellen!" He reached out to capture her hands, and Ellen backed away from him until she could go no further, for she felt the window seat behind her. The duke followed her relentlessly and took her hands in his.

"I have been wanting to talk to you this age!" he continued. "I beg you to listen, for I must tell you—it has become impossible to refrain from asking—and I am sure you have to admit..." He stopped in some confusion, and Lady Winship frowned a little, although her aunt Carleton would have had no trouble at all following the duke's deviations. Suddenly he took a deep breath and proclaimed, "My dearest Ellen, do me the honor of becoming my wife!"

Perhaps it was not the most polished of lovemaking, but it had the desired effect. Lady Winship gasped and sat down on the window seat abruptly, her face white, and the duke went down on one knee before her.

"I will try very hard not to speak to you in 'rehearsed periods,' like your young Lochinvar," he said fervently. "But I love you so much—much more than Carleton ever could! And I have loved you since the first time I saw you!"

Lady Winship sank back in the window embrasure. "No, no!" she said faintly. "It is Mariel you love, you know you do!"

"I have never loved Mariel!" the duke said firmly. "It was all to be near you, and when I saw that you thought I meant to ask for Mariel, I was in despair!"

"But she will be heartbroken!" Lady Winship said. "How could you be so unfeeling?"

He tightened his grip on her hands. "You will like to know, my love, that Mariel took me to task only this morning for not asking you to marry me! She has kindly consented to be my daughter, but she was horrified when I told her you wanted her to marry me. In fact, she said she could not believe it, for I was old; as old in fact as her father had been when he married you, and you had told her you would never force her into such a marriage!"

"But you are not in the least like Lord Braxton!" Lady Winship said in bewilderment. "Why, there is no comparison!"

The duke kissed her hands. "Thank you, my dear Ellen; that has done much to restore my somewhat battered self-esteem! You do see though, that to a young girl of seventeen, the comparison is most apt. To *you* I am not old, not now!"

"But Your Grace," she continued, determined to be practical, "you must marry someone who can preserve the name! I am thirty-five, you know!" This was said with such an air of gloom that the duke had to laugh as he rose and sat beside her.

"As for that, England is cluttered with Ainsworths! There must be hundreds of 'em, all wanting to be Duke of Chatham! My brother's eldest will do nicely—I like him, too!"

As Lady Winship lowered her eyes in confusion, he added, "Besides, do you envision us as Darby and Joan, my love? Sitting warmly wrapped in shawls in front of the fire, our gray heads nodding over some thin gruel, you with your cane, and I with my gouty foot? No such thing! We have years before we reach *that* stage, and I am sure we will enjoy them very much! Besides, we may surprise the world yet!"

Lady Winship blushed adorably. "I ... I do not know what to say, Your Grace!"

"Gregory!" the duke commanded, drawing her to her feet and putting his arms around her tenderly.

"Gregory, then!" Lady Winship said faintly. "But what will people think? And what of Lady Galley?"

The duke looked confused. "Janet? Why should she think anything of it at all? She will be delighted for she has been trying to get me to marry for many a year!"

"But she is so intimate with you...." Lady Winship persisted.

The duke's confusion vanished. "I should hope so, since she is my cousin and we were raised as brother and sister!"

Lady Winship was mortified by her late thoughts although she continued bravely, "But everyone in town thinks—I mean, you have been so particular in your attentions to Mariel that it will almost seem as if she had been jilted—and in her first season too! No, it is quite impossible!"

The duke sighed. "Let me tell you, my dear, that if I do not gain your consent very soon, the chances are excellent that Mariel will be betrothed before us!"

At Lady Winship's look of incomprehension he explained, "You see, right under your pretty nose, my dear, John Greeton has fallen in love with her. Although Mariel suspects it, he has not spoken as yet, but he is such a forceful, serious young man, I am sure he will not delay, nor will he accept a 'no' for her answer!"

"John Greeton?" Ellen asked faintly. "But I do not know his family, or his circumstances, or—oh dear, I had so hoped for a better connection for Mariel!"

The duke put his arms around her. "Yes, to a duke, no less, but that cock won't fight! Come, Ellen, Greeton was so good as to tell me that he has just inherited his great-uncle Malcolm's estate in Scotland, so you do know the family, and you must admit it more than a respectable match! And he does love her very much, for all her escapades, and that must weigh with you. And would you wager a guinea that the irresistible combination of a man who loves her—and Scotland too!—will tip the scales in his favor?"

Lady Winship shook her head. "I don't know . . . it is all too much . . . I must think!"

She put her hands against his chest and pushed, trying to get away, but the duke held her even more closely.

"Ellen!" he said in a commanding voice. "No, do not stare at my waistcoat, if you please! Look at me! Look at me and tell me if you can, that deep in your heart you do not love me!"

Ellen looked up, but what she saw in the duke's gray eyes stopped any further disclaimer. As she stared at him, those eyes grew even more intent, and before she knew what he was about, he bent his head and kissed her full on the lips. The kiss, which had begun gently, deepened in ardor, and although she meant to push him away, somehow she found her arms going around his neck, and she began to return his kiss. When he raised his head after a long moment, he gently kissed her forehead where the blond hair grew so charmingly, and murmured, "I have been wanting to kiss you there for so long! And here . . . and here . . ."

Ellen closed her eyes as the duke softly kissed her cheek and the little pulse in her throat. When he raised his head, he said unsteadily, "I will not carry you away across my saddlebow like young Lochinvar, my dearest, but I beg you not to delay our marriage for a moment longer than necessary! You do love me don't you, and you will marry me?"

Ellen smiled up at him happily, her eyes like green stars.

"I should be most pleased, Your Grace," she began formally, but that was all she was allowed to say before he began to kiss her again.

The butler, ear to the door in a very undignified way,

did not seem to be disappointed when the murmur of voices in the library ceased, and he nodded his head in satisfaction and went with slow measured steps to seek the housekeeper to impart some *very* interesting news!

FOURTEEN

That was not the only interesting news to develop that day, however. When John had finished his breakfast, he was in a much happier frame of mind than he had been for weeks, and he went at once to find Mariel now he was free to tell her of his love. Sometime later, however, he was becoming annoyed, for he had trudged through many a salon and drawing room, and down several long corridors, and she was nowhere to be found. He ran into Lady Carleton in the gallery, and she threw her arms around him and hugged him, beaming all the while, but when he questioned her, she refused to be drawn, only saying that she was sure there would be a surprise for them all today, just mark her words! John shook his head, wondering how she had guessed his secret, as he wandered into yet another room, vacant except for a small housemaid, engaged in polishing some brasses. Upon questioning her, she said as 'ow she 'adn't seen 'er ladyship, so he was no further along with his search.

He then had the happy thought that she might have gone to the stables, and even if she had gone for a ride, at least he would be there when she returned, and he could speak without further delay. He went out a side door and found Algy pacing up and down the terrace looking miserable.

"I say, Algy!" he asked. "You haven't seen Mariel about, have you?" Even to his own ears, his tone of voice when he spoke her name was a dead giveaway to his feelings, but Algy did not appear to notice.

"No, I have not!" his friend snapped. "And if you had any sense at all, man, you would avoid that one at all costs! It has been some time since the curricle race; she must be planning some more deviltry by now, even marooned here in the country! What she needs is someone to take a strong hand with her—not that anyone that foolish could be found to volunteer!" He laughed harshly.

John found himself flushing. "You must not speak of her so, Algy, for I intend to be the one who supplies the 'strong hand' you mention! You see, I love her, and I intend to marry her!"

"YOU?" Algy asked in disbelief. "You are in love with Mariel?"

John had to laugh at his incredulous tone. "Come, wish me luck Algy, and I pray you will soon be wishing me happy!"

Algy shook his friend by the hand. "I shall certainly wish you happy if that is your bent, John, but you must forgive me for saying that if I were you, I would even now be planning an immediate voyage to the other end of the earth! Women! There is not a one of 'em that I would waste a moment's time on! I, for one, shall never marry!" He sighed deeply, for his mother had told him in passing that morning that she expected the duke to offer for Ellen that very day, and Algy was feeling very depressed and somewhat betrayed. He was only waiting, he told John mournfully, for his bags to be packed, and then he was off to London at once! John pressed his hand in sympathy and clapped him on the shoulder before he ran down the steps and across the lawn to the stableyard.

The head groom admitted that Lady Mary Ellen had indeed gone for a ride but had promised to return by lunchtime, and with this John had to be content. He strolled back to the house, happily breathing the fresh summer air, so charmingly scented with roses. It was a beautiful day, he thought, and was sure to become even more so!

In the meantime, Mariel was sitting in a small clearing in the duke's park, her horse grazing nearby on some lush grass. She thought of everything the duke had told her that morning and shook her head a little that her mother should be so blind as to think her at all attracted to such an older man as Ainsworth, nice though he was. When she compared him to John, for example—but then she put that thought firmly from her head. She had told the duke she had no wish to marry, and she had meant it, she told herself stoutly. MEN! She did not see of what use they were, and she had never really believed John when he had said he wanted her to be his wife. Why, that was weeks ago, and he had never said another word about it! Of course, she told herself honestly as she picked a daisy near her feet and proceeded to strip off its petals, that might be because I was careful never to see him alone, but no! If he had really wanted to marry me, it was his *duty* to speak up, long before this! Perhaps he is sorry he spoke so rashly that day of the race, she thought gloomily, and in thinking it over has decided to beat a hasty retreat. But then last night at the ball, she reminded herself, he had looked at her in such a way—and had told her how beautiful she was—and she had often seen him watching her as she danced! But when she had come to sit with him after waltzing with the duke, and yes—they were quite alone then!—he had been so stiff, so formal! She sighed. It was a quandary, but what a good thing she had decided that she did not wish to marry anyone! She rose and dusted off her habit with a great air of decision and putting up her chin, went to fetch her horse. As soon as the duke and her mother had set their wedding date, perhaps they would leave Chatham Park for town, for she knew Lady Carleton would insist on a great amount of shopping before the festivities. She was not exactly sure if second marriages required bridal clothes, but knowing her aunt, there was sure to be shopping! And then perhaps, at long last, she would be able to return to Lochcrae.

As she turned the horse's head for home, she wondered why she felt so sad and unhappy, when just the thought of returning to Lochcrae should have filled her with joy. She decided that her spirits were sure to improve the closer she got to home and Uncle James! And, she told herself firmly as she kicked the mare to a canter, I shall be very definite to mama and the duke about living with Uncle James and never coming to town again for I have hated the London season and find the whole silly thing insipid! She felt much better after making this decision, and when she reached the stableyard, dismounted quickly. The clock in the tower there told her she had stayed away longer than she should, and the others would even now be preparing to sit down to one of the duke's delicious luncheons. She decided to take the time to change into one of her prettiest new gowns, a soft yellow muslin with tiny sleeves and white satin flowers embroidered at random all over the material. She had some slippers to match, she remembered, as she went in a little used side door that she had discovered allowed her to reach her room much more quickly than going around to the front and up the massive stairs. Of course in doing so she missed John, who was patiently waiting for her in the hall, much to the surprise of the butler who wondered what on earth the young man was hanging about for!

She joined the others at the table a few minutes later in a very subdued frame of mind and went to give her mother a kiss. Lady Winship looked so radiantly happy, and the duke so proud, that she felt a lump in her throat, and for a moment felt she might disgrace herself by bursting into tears. She did not dare to look at John as she went to the duke to shake his hand.

"I—I wish you very happy, Your Grace!" she said stiffly, but the duke would have none of such formality, and swept her up in his arms for a hug and a kiss, saying that from someone who was soon to be so closely related, he expected more warmth!

Lady Carleton beamed. "Yes, it will be good for Mariel to have a father's influence! You must keep a very close eye on her you know, Ainsworth!"

Mariel stole a look at John as she took her seat, and found him staring at her; yes, positively staring! She flushed as the duke said, "Perhaps I will not be in a position of authority for long, Lady Carleton, for Mariel is sure to be married before much longer!"

"I do not intend to ever marry, not ever!" Mariel said firmly, staring into a glass of champagne the butler had just poured for her, and wishing she might quietly slip under the table and disappear forever. This was much worse than she had imagined it would be! The duke, catching sight of John's strained face and the little shake of his head, deftly turned the subject.

"But come! Let us drink to the future Duchess of Chatham!" he said, raising his glass to Lady Winship, his eyes glowing. "To my dearest Ellen!"

"Hear, hear!" John replied valiantly as everyone joined in the toast.

"What a shame that Algy had to leave for town so precipitously!" Lady Carleton said. "I shall never understand the young, never! Dashing off to London like that, with hardly a moment's notice!"

The duke and Ellen exchanged thankful glances, happy to be spared Algy's presence, the specter at the feast. For them and for Lady Carleton, it was a joyous luncheon that sped by with much laughter and many toasts and plans, but to Mariel and John, it seemed endless. When at last it was over, and they all rose to leave the dining room, he hastened to her side.

"I must speak to you, Mariel! I have been searching for you all morning! Where the *devil* did you get to?"

Mariel stiffened. What business was it of his where she had been? Moreover, he had not thought to search very hard, for she had not gone riding until quite late in the morning.

"You must excuse me, Mr. Greeton," she said haughtily. "As for where I have been, I must remind you again that that is none of your concern! Now, if you will be so good as to allow me to pass..."

She put up her chin and made to follow the others who were now at the door to the hall, but John took her arm in his good hand in a hard grip and said between his teeth, "No you don't!" He had been much upset to hear her state so finally that she never intended to marry at the luncheon table, for he was sure he knew his Mariel. This quiet, formal miss was a new come-out indeed! He was so completely exasperated by this new turn of events that he shook her a little, and added, "What ever is the matter with you? 'None of my concern' indeed! I'll take none of your sass, my girl!"

Mariel was indignant. How dare he? Before she could frame a blistering set-down, he added more gently, "If you knew what was in my heart, my dear marigold, you would not be so cruel!"

For a moment she wavered, but then she tossed her head. "You may say what you have to say right here, sir, for I see you intend to force me to accede to your wishes!"

John looked wildly around the dining room. At the sideboard, the butler appeared completely deaf and indifferent to the scene, but the two footmen engaged in clearing the table were having a hard time trying to emulate such *sangfroid*. He reddened, and shook her again. "What do you mean, 'right here'? A man cannot propose in front of a parcel of servants!"

"Propose?" Mariel asked, as if she had never heard the word before, although her heart was beating wildly in her breast. "Oh, you mean you have caught the fever, sir, seeing my mother and the duke all April and May! Please do not trouble yourself! I meant what I said— I do not intend to marry, ever! In a short time I am for Scotland—alone!"

John was beginning to look extremely harassed as she pulled away from him and went swiftly into the hall. The others had disappeared, and she ran to the front door to escape, followed closely by John, to the amazement of a passing footman, who bowed and opened the door for them. Nodding her thanks, she ran down the steps to the drive, leaving the footman to shake his head and mutter about the crazy ways of the quality!

"Mariel, wait!" she heard from behind her, and the closeness of John's voice made her increase her pace. She headed for the lake, thinking she might reach the boat before he caught her up and row out to the gazebo on the little island in the middle where she could indulge in a good cry, for her eyes were already beginning to fill with tears.

Unfortunately, her flight disturbed a pair of swans who were resting with their new family in some reeds near the shore, and as one they rose up hissing and came after her, their long white necks swaying with their anger at this intrusion so near their nest. John saw what was happening and increased his speed.

"Mariel!" he called more urgently. "The swans!"

But she had already seen them and was considerably frightened. She only hoped she could manage to get an oar which she could use to defend herself. Thank heavens they were such ungainly birds on land, she thought after a quick look over her shoulder. She reached the boat just ahead of the cob and threw herself into it. The swan stopped at the edge of the lake and hissed angrily again, and Mariel, who thought he looked cross enough to try to come into the boat after her, seized an oar. Unfortunately, she stepped on the hem of her gown as she rose to do battle, and the boat, now swinging wildly, tipped over and spilled her into the lake.

John arrived just as the astonished swans were about to ready their attack again, this time on more familiar territory, and pulling in a floating oar, he beat about him until he had them waddling away in defeat.

On the terrace, the duke detained his bride-to-be with a firm hand. "No, my love! She cannot possibly drown, for the water is only a few feet deep there, and see, John is going to save her! Come, let us retreat behind this urn where we cannot be seen and watch the end of this mad wooing! I wish young Greeton well, for Mariel is sure to be as mad as a ... as a wet hen!"

Ellen allowed herself to be persuaded when he put his arms around her and drew her behind the urn.

John, in the meantime, stood on the shores of the lake and stared at the girl he loved, rising up from the water covered with water lilies and mud, her new gown sopping wet and her carefully arranged curls dripping damply all over her face and down her back, and he was hard put not to laugh. Instead, he held out the oar gravely, as she floundered over a stone on the bottom and went back to her knees again.

"Here, Mariel, take hold of this, and I will pull you to shore!" he commanded.

Mariel realized she would only look ridiculous if she refused his offer, for her feet were entangled in some water lily roots, and she knew she could not get free without help. She grasped the oar with both hands, and throwing off his sling, John pulled her to shore. Dropping the oar, he reached down and helped her up the bank.

"My love!" he said fondly, pulling her into his arms, completely indifferent to her wet, dripping gown and muddy face.

At that, Mariel burst into tears and sobbed as if her heart would break. John patted her and held her close, murmuring endearments while seeming to be delighted to be so thoroughly dampened in the process, until her crying died away into a few sniffles and an occasional hiccup.

"Dearest Mariel!" he said when at last she was calm and was resting her head on what had been a sparkling white cravat only a short time before. He tipped up her chin and looked down into her eyes.

"Now, m'lady, with no further ado, I have the honor to ask you to be my bride!"

Mariel tried weakly to get away. "No, no!" she exclaimed, beginning to cry again. "You do not really want to marry me! It has been weeks since the curricle race, and not one inkling have you let slip of your intentions since then! I fear you are being gallant because we were alone at the inn for so long, and now you are thinking I might be depressed because the duke is marrying my mother, and have been so kind as to offer for me, but it will not do! Besides," she added darkly, "you cannot propose when I look like this!"

John was understandably impatient with this line of reasoning, and said hotly, "And I am to contain myself for over an hour after waiting all morning until you are changed and with every curl in place? No, not another minute will I wait! And let me point out to you, my dearest idiot, a gentleman does not propose to a lady because she is depressed! I only hesitated to do so because you avoided me so much I was sure you were in love with the duke! It was only after I spoke to him this morning that I felt free to ask you, for I have always loved you!"

"You have?" she asked wonderingly. "Really? You do mean it, in spite of all my bad behavior?"

"Darling!" John said fondly. "Of course I have! How could I help it, my adorable marigold!"

Mariel chuckled. "A very *wet* marigold, John!" she said regretfully

"You look like a flower after a spring rain!" he replied, more poetically than truthfully, as he removed a dripping water lily from behind her ear.

Mariel peeped up at him with delight. His hazel eyes were smiling down at her so warmly, with such a fond light in them, and his arms were so comfortingly close around her, that she had to sigh a little in contentment, and John, rightfully interpreting this little sign, bent his head and kissed her.

When at last he took his warm lips from hers and raised his head, she sighed again, this time a sigh of pure delight.

221

"I never knew it would be like that!" she said naively, which only caused him to kiss her again.

"But you have not asked where we are to live, Mariel," John said at last. "Suppose I insist that we buy a town house and spend all our time in London?"

Mariel swallowed hard. "If... if you want to live in town, John, then that is where we will live!" She tried to smile reassuringly at him as he hugged her.

"I am teasing you, my love. You said you were for Scotland—what a coincidence! Will you be pleased to know that I am going there too? But not alone, my love, not alone! I intend to bring you as my bride to Rook's Place!"

Mariel leaned back in his arms and stared at him. "But John!" she said in a shocked voice. "That is Lord Malcolm's estate, near Lochcrae!"

"Lord Malcolm was my great-uncle—he died this spring and I find he made me his heir! Does that please you, Mariel? I do not intend to be like Lord Lawrence you know, spending most of my time with the ton! In fact, I am hoping that your Uncle James will be kind enough to help me get settled in my new role, for I have never farmed in Scotland!"

"Oh John, my dearest John!" Mariel exclaimed happily. "Scotland—and you too! I do not deserve such happiness!"

He laughed and kissed her again, and to the interested couple on the terrace, lurking behind an urn, it was all most satisfying. They saw Mariel's arms steal up around John's neck and watched as they embraced for a very long time. Ellen smiled.

"So you were right, my dear, and she is in love with John after all! I wish them happy, indeed I do!"

The duke smiled down at her. "As happy as we shall be, my love! And may I say that I can only be grateful that you are not given to falling into ponds just before a proposal? How very uncomfortable it must be to hold a dripping wet lady with any degree of delight and composure! I must make my compliments to young Greeton!"

He went to summon the butler to bring more champagne to the terrace so they might toast the young couple, as Ellen dreamily watched her daughter and John slowly make their way up the lawn to the terrace, stopping often to smile at each other and exchange another kiss. When they saw her there, they waved and hurried towards her, and she recalled a line from Scot as she went down the steps to greet them and wish them happy, and murmured softly to herself, "For love will still be lord of all!"

Let COVENTRY Give You
A Little Old-Fashioned Romance

☐ LADY BRANDY   50165 $1.75
   by Claudette Williams

☐ THE SWANS OF BRHYADR   50166 $1.75
   by Vivienne Couldrey

☐ HONORA CLARE   50167 $1.75
   by Sheila Bishop

☐ TWIST OF CHANCE   50169 $1.75
   by Elisabeth Carey

☐ THE RELUCTANT RIVALS   50170 $1.75
   by Georgina Grey

☐ THE MERCHANT'S
   DAUGHTER   50172 $1.75
   by Rachelle Edwards

Buy them at your local bookstore or use this handy coupon for ordering.

COLUMBIA BOOK SERVICE (a CBS Publications Co.)
32275 Mally Road, P.O. Box FB, Madison Heights, MI 48071

Please send me the books I have checked above. Orders for less than 5 books must include 75¢ for the first book and 25¢ for each additional book to cover postage and handling. Orders for 5 books or more postage is FREE. Send check or money order only.

Cost $ _____	Name _____
Sales tax* _____	Address _____
Postage _____	City _____
Total $ _____	State _____ Zip _____

The government requires us to collect sales tax in all states except AK, DE, MT, NH and OR.

This offer expires 1 December 81.   8136